That's My Baby!

Celia was a natural mother.

A strange sensation churned inside Hunter, as if a giant fist was twisting his insides into knots.

"I'd like to give J.J. a pony of his own as a birthday present," she said. "If you don't mind." She smiled eagerly, looking like a young girl, happy and beautiful and full of life.

He gazed at her very plump middle. His heart acted odd—sort of jumping around in his chest as if excited. His wife *was* full of life…with his child. Their child. A daughter.

"Maybe we could buy it together," he offered hesitantly.

"Oh, that would be good. He'd like that. It would be like a real family."

Like a real family. The words drummed in his brain. There was the key to their future. But the question was, could he ever be a real husband to this woman he'd so precipitously married?

Dear Reader,

Autumn inspires visions of the great outdoors, but Special Edition lures you back inside with six vibrant romances!

Many of the top-selling mainstream authors today launched their careers writing series romance. Some special authors have achieved remarkable success in the mainstream with both hardcovers and paperbacks, yet continue to support the genre and the readers they love. *New York Times* bestselling author Nora Roberts is just such an author, and this month we're delighted to bring you *The Winning Hand*, the eighth book in her popular series THE MACGREGORS.

In *Father-to-Be* by Laurie Paige, October's tender THAT'S MY BABY! title, an impulsive night of passion changes a rugged rancher's life forever. And if you enjoy sweeping medical dramas, we prescribe *From House Calls to Husband* by Christine Flynn, part of PRESCRIPTION: MARRIAGE. This riveting new series by three Silhouette authors highlights nurses who vow never to marry a doctor. Look for the second installment of the series next month.

Silhouette's new five-book cross-line continuity series, FOLLOW THAT BABY, introduces the Wentworth oil tycoon family and their search for a missing heir. The series begins in Special Edition this month with *The Rancher and the Amnesiac Bride* by Joan Elliott Pickart, then crosses into Romance (11/98), Desire (12/98), Yours Truly (1/99) and concludes in Intimate Moments (2/99).

Also, check out *Partners in Marriage* by Allison Hayes, in which a vulnerable schoolteacher invades a Lakota man's house—and his heart! Finally, October's WOMAN TO WATCH is talented newcomer Jean Brashear, who unfolds a provocative tale of revenge—and romance—in *The Bodyguard's Bride*.

I hope you enjoy all of the stories this month!

Sincerely,

Karen Taylor Richman
Senior Editor

Please address questions and book requests to:
Silhouette Reader Service
U.S.: 3010 Walden Ave., P.O. Box 1325, Buffalo, NY 14269
Canadian: P.O. Box 609, Fort Erie, Ont. L2A 5X3

LAURIE PAIGE

FATHER-TO-BE

Silhouette®

SPECIAL EDITION®

Published by Silhouette Books

America's Publisher of Contemporary Romance

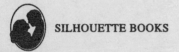 SILHOUETTE BOOKS

ISBN 0-373-24201-8

FATHER-TO-BE

Books by Laurie Paige

Silhouette Special Edition

Lover's Choice #170
Man Without a Past #755
*Home for a Wild Heart #828
*A Place for Eagles #839
*The Way of a Man #849
*Wild Is the Wind #887
*A River To Cross #910
Molly Darling #1021
Live-In Mom #1077
The Ready-Made Family #1114
*Husband: Bought and
Paid For* #1139
†A Hero's Homecoming #1178
Warrior's Woman #1193
Father-To-Be #1201

Silhouette Desire

Gypsy Enchantment #123
Journey to Desire #195
Misty Splendor #304
Golden Promise #404

Silhouette Yours Truly

Christmas Kisses for a Dollar
Only One Groom Allowed

‡All-American Sweethearts
*Wild River
†Montana Mavericks:
  Return to Whitehorn

Silhouette Romance

South of the Sun #296
A Tangle of Rainbows #333
A Season for Butterflies #364
Nothing Lost #382
The Sea at Dawn #398
A Season for Homecoming #727
Home Fires Burning Bright #733
Man from the North Country #772
‡Cara's Beloved #917
‡Sally's Beau #923
‡Victoria's Conquest #933
Caleb's Son #994
*A Rogue's Heart #1013
An Unexpected Delivery #1151
Wanted: One Son #1246
The Guardian's Bride #1318

Silhouette Books

Montana Mavericks

The Once and Future Wife
Father Found

LAURIE PAIGE

was recently presented with the *Affaire de Coeur* Readers' Choice Silver Pen Award for Favorite Contemporary Author. In addition, she was a 1994 Romance Writers of America (RITA) finalist for Best Traditional Romance for her book *Sally's Beau*. She reports romance is blooming in her part of northern California. With the birth of her second grandson, she finds herself madly in love with three wonderful males—"all hero material." So far, her husband hasn't complained about the other men in her life.

Dear Reader,

I firmly believe, along with Ms. Austen, that every man in possession of a good fortune should have a wife. After writing the story of Hunter's brother, I just couldn't bear it that Hunter was alone—a man with a son he loved more than his own life but wasn't sure how to reach. Obviously, he needed help. He needed a wife.

Who would be the best mate for him?

I wanted someone special, someone different from his first love, someone who could bring him back to living his life to its fullest. I also wanted someone special for J.J., a lonely little boy who felt abandoned by the mother who had died when he was hardly more than a baby.

This is what I enjoy most about writing romance stories—bringing together two people who are perfect for each other...only they don't know it yet. Then I like to stir in children, family and friends in a wonderfully frustrating mix of well-meaning but unsought advice, plus a healthy dollop of emotion, and watch what happens. And when you have a couple madly in love and a child who needs them both, then you have the most miraculous thing—a family!

Laurie Paige

Chapter One

"**Y**ou're what?"

"Pregnant." Cecilia Campbell—"Celia," as she preferred to be known, rather than the childish "Sissy" she'd been stuck with all of her growing years—maintained her happy smile with an effort.

Hunter McLean, the man who had so generously and graciously, not to mention passionately, given her the birthday wish she'd asked for, was no longer the surprised-but-congenial host he'd been when she'd appeared at his door fifteen minutes ago to tell him the news.

His eyes took on a frosty glare. His dark eyebrows drew into an ominous V. His hands—hands that had touched her with amazing gentleness and caressed her until she'd wept with pleasure—bunched into fists at his sides. He looked downright dangerous at this moment.

"Two months," she added needlessly.

As if he wouldn't remember New Year's Eve and the dinner dance at the country club. She and Adam, the local vet and an old school chum, had been worried about him because he'd had too much to drink; hence her offer to drive him home. She'd taken him to her house because the roads were icy and it was a long way to the ranch. They'd ended up sipping cocoa by the fire with the radio softly playing.

Her breath knotted in her throat as she remembered what had happened next. At midnight, hearing the fireworks and horns that heralded the New Year, Hunter had kissed her.

She pressed a hand to her fast-beating heart as she experienced again that odd, tingly glow that had swept through her at the touch of his lips. It had been almost painful in its intensity as old feelings rose to haunt her. This was Hunter, her first love. Once she'd dreamed he would love her, too. Once, so very long ago...

When the kiss had ended, it had been January first. Her birthday.

Seduced by the camaraderie of their shared confidences and the longing generated by the soul-stirring kiss, she'd told him this fact and explained her wish for a child because she was thirty and not getting any younger... Well, he'd agreed.

She watched him warily when he pushed away from the kitchen counter and took a step toward her. She sat up straighter in the limed-oak chair and kept her head high, her smile in place.

Celia didn't like it when people frowned. It made her nervous. Her childhood had been rife with frowns since her parents had quarreled constantly. It was no secret to her that she had been an unwanted child. Her parents had been forced to marry because of her impending birth.

She looped her arms protectively over her abdomen. It wouldn't be like that for this baby. She wanted it with everything in her. Her child had been conceived in passion; it would be born in love and joy and—

"And?" he said, his green eyes—eyes to die for, as all the girls at school used to say—never leaving her face.

It sounded like a trick question. She would have preferred something friendlier.

I'm happy for you.... I'd like to hear more....

There were lots of other things he could say, but judging by the ice particles in his gaze, she was beginning to think none of them would be pleasant.

She tugged at her wool miniskirt. She'd chosen her clothing carefully for this expedition. Blue was supposed to be men's favorite color, she'd once read. She'd acted on that assumption.

Her sweater was blue, the skirt was a blue, black, gray and burgundy plaid. She wore a short cape that matched the skirt and had chosen black tights and boots to finish the outfit. She had thought it stylish and yet practical for the last week in February.

Winters in the Sierra Nevada of northern California could be brutally cold. Today was no exception. The thermometer hovered at twenty-five degrees.

However, there was no wind and the sun was shining, so the day was bright and brisk and altogether pleasant. It had been a week since the last snow, so the roads were clear.

Since all the signs were propitious, she had decided to tell Hunter the news right away. Up until this moment, she had felt wonderful.

"And I wanted to thank you. It was my birthday, you may remember, and, well, I explained it all to you. Anyway, I'm thrilled. I had always assumed I would have children by now. I wanted two—a boy and a girl—but I didn't really think— I mean, a child on the first try and all... I thought you might like to know," she finished brightly, her face hot and strained from hanging on to the smile.

"There's something I'm not getting, here," Hunter remarked, folding his arms across his chest.

He was a rancher of Scots and German stock, with maybe a little Viking thrown in. His ancestors had settled in the area a hundred and thirty years ago. He stood a couple of inches over six feet without his boots, his chest was brawny, his arms and legs were lashed with muscles that had felt like hardened steel to her exploring fingers.

For a moment, she remembered the wonder of touching him, of running her hands all over his big, masculine body, of knowing his strength on terms so intimate that, if the child growing inside her hadn't provided proof, she still wouldn't have believed she had made love with Hunter McLean.

Heat swept over her. Electricity arced through her—

"Well?" Hunter snapped, causing her to start.

"Well, uh, that's all."

She stood and smoothed her skirt down. He hadn't

liked her outfit at all, and she had so wanted to make a good impression. After all, he was the father of her child, which he obviously didn't care about in the least.

"I'd better run—appointments and people to see, you know. Ta-ta." She wiggled her fingers at him and headed for the door, wanting only to escape the awkward scene and his disturbing presence. He seemed on the verge of exploding and she didn't want to be around when it happened.

Hunter caught up with her in one long stride, his hand clasping her wrist and bringing her to a halt. Her heart fluttered nervously as he leaned close.

"Are you trying to tell me I'm the father?" he asked incredulously, the sharp sting of denial in his words.

She stared up at him, feeling like a time-traveler caught in some surreal moment when nothing made sense. He gave her arm a little shake.

"Yes," she said. "Of course. That's why I came out here. I mean, I read this article in a magazine and it said you should let the father know right away, that it was only fair to both him and the child, that men deserve a place in their children's lives and women often try to close them out. My mother did that to my father. I didn't want to do it to you...."

She knew she was rattling on. She did that sometimes when she got nervous.

Nervous?

She was trembling like the proverbial leaf in the teeth of a gale. When she pulled back, he released her and folded his arms over his chest again, as forbidding as a wall of granite rimed with ice.

She blinked up at him, wishing she'd worn platform shoes so she wouldn't appear so much shorter than him; but she'd worn two-inch-heeled boots because she didn't want to teeter around and maybe fall and hurt the baby.

His jaw worked as if he was gritting his teeth.

She really wished she hadn't followed the advice in that magazine.

"Why the hell did you pick me to be the father?"

Another trick question?

She could answer it. Only the fact that he was the handsomest man she'd ever known, that she'd been half in love with him her entire life, that she knew him to be a person of honor and integrity, and that he was fair-minded and possessed a sense of humor—usually. Those factors had caused her to choose him.

"Well, I know you. That's one reason—"

"That's a relief," he muttered sarcastically. "At least you didn't go down to the local bar and pick out a total stranger to pin the rap on."

Pin the rap on? It was her turn to be incredulous. "Why would I do something like that?"

"Beats me."

Hunter had been in his socks when he'd greeted her at the door and let her into the house. Even without boots, he towered over her, looking down at her as if he were an enraged colossus and she, an insignificant human he was thinking of crushing.

"Wait a minute," she said, a sinking feeling in her middle. "Do you think… Do you think that I…that you're not…that I'm lying?"

"If the shoe fits, honey," he suggested in that particularly nasty male way that drove women to think of arsenic for the next batch of brownies.

He didn't believe her at all!

It came as shocking news, the way a terrible tragedy leaps upon the senses, leaving her devastated by the loss and feeling helpless to cope.

Pride came to her rescue. She stretched to her full five feet four inches and gave him her mother's haughtiest glare. "I haven't been seriously involved in a relationship for the past five years."

Involved? She hadn't dated at all, other than two boring dinners a friend had arranged. The one serious affair had ended when her steady and her mother had engaged in a shouting match. She'd realized the two were very much alike in temperament and Celia didn't want to be married to someone who reminded her of her mother.

His grin was openly skeptical. "Are you saying you haven't been with any man since you were twenty-five until this latest...?" He waved his hand vaguely to indicate her present condition.

"I don't sleep around."

"If that's all the experience you're claiming to have, sleep is about *all* you've done."

"It was a mistake coming here." She moved to the kitchen door. "I'm sorry to have bothered you."

"Hold on. I want to understand something, here."

She watched him warily. Her mother had distrusted men since her father had run off with another woman—actually, with Hunter's aunt—fourteen years ago. Celia could appreciate the sentiment. She didn't know exactly what she'd expected from Hunter, but this denial was too much.

Why, he acted as if he'd never even touched her.

"What?" she prompted when he didn't speak but continued to scrutinize her with flames sizzling in his green eyes.

Not the flames of passion that had blazed there on New Year's Eve, she recalled with a sense of sadness.

They'd shared so much that night. He'd told her of his loneliness and how much he missed April—his wife, his love. She'd wanted so desperately to comfort him, to fill the empty spots in his life that were so like her own. They had clung to each other in grief; then, wonder of wonders, they had welcomed the New Year in each other's arms.

Well, no use getting poetical about it. She had to be practical, now that she was to be a mother.

A tiny thrill echoed through her as it did each time she thought of the coming child. A baby. Dear God. She closed her eyes as the joy of it swept over her yet again.

"You're not going to faint, are you?"

The irascible growl broke into her heady delight. She opened her eyes. "Of course not."

Hunter looked so angry. Just like her parents when they'd quarreled.

She swallowed the lump that filled her throat. His denial jarred her right down to her toes. In all the sweet, silly daydreams that had come to her during the drive out to the McLean ranch, none of them had included this.

She'd thought he would be pleased that he'd granted her the cherished birthday wish she'd asked for. It wasn't as if she'd tricked him. She'd asked and he'd agreed.

Even more stupid, she'd dreamed that he might realize he'd fallen in love with her, sweep her into his arms and demand that they marry right away.

Not that she'd thought that for longer than a split second. No, of course not. But it would have been nice if he'd acted pleased.

"I'd like to go, Hunter."

"Answer me one question first."

She nodded.

"Did you really think you could get away with a paternity suit in this day and age?"

"It's your child, Hunter. I don't know why you're saying it isn't."

He heaved an exasperated sigh. "Sissy, I haven't made love to a woman since my wife died."

"Don't call me Sissy," she automatically corrected. The implication of his statement hit her. "Oh. Then it had been a long time for you, too. I'm glad. I thought I was just one more in a long line of Hunter McLean conquests."

Her heart, ever the optimist, fluttered a bit at his news. Maybe her dreams weren't so crazy...

"Am I not speaking English?" he asked, peering upward at the ceiling. He speared her with a chilly gaze. "I have not been with a woman since April died," he repeated.

"You were with me—"

"Dammit, don't you think I'd remember it?" he demanded, cutting off her words.

She stared at him, aghast. "You don't remember?"

"No." He folded his arms again. "Why don't you refresh my memory of this mysterious night of passion we shared?"

Her stomach lurched. She clenched a fist and pressed it to her middle. She was not going to have morning sickness here in front of Hunter when he was being so arrogantly male. To lose her breakfast would be the ultimate indignity.

"It was New Year's Eve," she managed to say. Her jaw was so tight she could hardly speak. "My thirtieth birthday was the next day. I was the first baby born that year in the county. They wrote it up in the papers."

"Huh," he said, sounding skeptical even about that.

"I had always planned to start my family by now. I thought I would be married and…and happy. Prince Charming and all that."

She paused in sympathy for that very young and foolish girl of long ago who, in spite of her parents' marriage, had thought her life would be different.

Her stomach heaved again. She should have eaten something after leaving the doctor's office. She'd been so anxious to share her wonderful news that she hadn't thought of food or anything.

"Go on."

"Well, I mentioned all this to you. I asked if you'd be willing to, uh… And you agreed and, uh, then…"

"I did the dastardly deed," he supplied.

"No," she said, trying to be perfectly honest and up-front about the whole affair. Not that it had been an affair. It had most definitely been a one-night stand. "You were wonderful. I was nervous, but you knew exactly what to do. I mean, everything went fine," she ended lamely.

Words were a tepid substitute for what had happened between them. Wild eroticism. Heated passion. Mind-boggling excitement. Tension. Then release.

After that, she'd experienced the most perfect contentment. Like floating in a warm sea. Love and happiness and a deep, deep serenity that reached right into the soul.

None of it real.

"Let me tell you what I remember. There was the dance, yes. I had a few drinks, but couldn't seem to get drunk enough to forget—" He broke off, then shook his head as if clearing a bad memory. "I don't remember anything after that. I woke up in my bed the next day with a hell of a headache. That's my memory of the night."

"You danced with me."

He nodded. "I could have. I vaguely remember music."

"We danced and talked some about things we had wanted from life. You drifted away. Later, Adam took your car keys when you decided to leave. You were arguing about it. I had ridden over with friends, so I volunteered to drive you home, only we went to my place because the roads were icy." She stopped and peered up at him anxiously.

There was no spark of remembrance in his eyes, only a pitying sort of distrust, as if he couldn't imagine why she'd make up such a tale.

Her stomach tried to turn itself inside out. She swallowed and held on until the spasm passed. The morning sickness was just starting. So far, it had been awful. She'd rather die than succumb in front of Hunter.

"That's all," she finished hurriedly. She had to get

out of here. "Never mind, Hunter. You're right. It couldn't have been you. Sorry to have imposed."

A movement jerked her attention to the doorway into the hall. Hunter's son stood there, his hair tousled as if he'd just got out of bed. His cheeks were flushed with fever. Each breath he took rattled with the raspy sound of a cold. He watched her with a curious expression in his eyes.

For an odd second, she felt as if she'd found a kindred spirit, someone who was sad inside....

Hunter followed her gaze. His frown softened. "This is J.J.," he said. "My son." He lifted the boy into his arms and faced her. "This is the only child I've ever sired."

They stood there in a frozen tableau, then she shook her head helplessly. This time when she headed out, he let her go. A big black dog bounded across the lawn and sniffed at her ankles. Terrified, she broke into a run.

She jumped into her car and drove off quickly, leaving Hunter McLean and his brute of a dog far behind. She sighed with relief at her escape.

The cool air calmed the nausea and she made without mishap the journey to the town near Honey Lake and the house she'd inherited a year ago from her grandmother.

She was older and wiser by far on the return trip than on the trip out. She'd never heed the advice in a magazine again.

Neither would she make the mistake of thinking there could ever be anything other than that one night of fleeting passion between her and Hunter. He hadn't looked her way in the past, and only a fool would dream they could have a future.

An image of Hunter and his son pushed its way into her mind. Father and son, so much alike with their dark hair and incredible eyes, although J.J.'s eyes were blue, as his mother's had been, rather than green.

Celia's heart lurched painfully as she wondered who her child would resemble.

Pregnant.

The word beat through Hunter's head. He couldn't believe Sissy had had the nerve to try an old trick like that. She wasn't an Einstein, but even she should know a man wouldn't fall for that in this age of modern science.

It made absolutely no sense.

Unless...

No.

Hell, no. Nothing had happened that night.

He'd knocked back a couple of glasses of champagne, then a couple of Scotches—okay, maybe three—but he'd been far from senseless, although he'd wanted oblivion.

It had been on New Year's Eve six years ago that he had asked April to marry him. She'd been gone a little over two years, killed when the cattle truck driven by her father had overturned.

Forty-six months of bliss and twenty-seven of hell. He'd wanted to die, too, for a long time after her death.

The holiday, along with their wedding day and the day she'd died, were all dates he wanted to forget.

That was why he'd gone to the country club. To forget.

Judging by the evidence of the empty Scotch bottle on the kitchen counter at the ranch, he'd done his drinking in the safety of his home after he'd returned from the dance. He could vaguely recall entering the silent house—J.J. and his mother had been asleep—and opening a full bottle. In it, he'd finally found the oblivion he'd sought.

That was the extent of his memories.

A sudden image leaped into his consciousness. A woman. Touching him, her hands gentle, her voice a soft, sexy croon of delight. Whose hands? Whose voice?

He tried to see her, but he couldn't. There were only the caresses and the voice....

Shaken, he helped J.J. into his winter coat, mittens and hat and headed outside. He needed air and a sense of space around him. Sissy's accusation was playing havoc with his mind. At the paddock, he leaned against the railing and watched his son pull grass and feed it to one of the mares that came over to investigate. J.J.'s black Lab cavorted around the boy, happy to have him outside again.

Recently, the doctors at the clinic down in Reno had diagnosed his son as borderline autistic—whatever that meant. Hunter rubbed a hand over his aching forehead.

His son didn't talk. The sounds he'd made before April had died had stopped and never been repeated after her death. The boy had withdrawn into himself. The doctors were divided on how bad it was and on a course of treatment.

Figuring out what to do about this problem was enough complication in his life. And now this thing with Sissy Campbell—

"Why so angry?" a feminine voice inquired.

Hunter shifted his stance, turning to his right as Dawn came up to the paddock railing and leaned against it. She bent and dropped a smacking kiss on J.J., earning one of the kid's few and solemn smiles.

She was his sister-in-law—first because she was his wife's sister, then because she'd married his half brother last fall. She was a long cool drink of a woman; tall, slender, a blue-eyed Nordic blonde. Beautiful.

As April had been.

Sissy Campbell was short—barely up to his shoulder in height—and although not plump, definitely curvy. She had a gamine face with a trace of freckles across her nose and cheeks, brown eyes, hair that was sort of light brown with red highlights and blond streaks.

For a second, he saw again the bright expectancy that had been on her face when she'd first arrived— as if she anticipated nothing but good things from life. When she'd left, the smile had lingered, but the sparkle had faded. He shrugged off a flicker of guilt.

"Not so much angry as puzzled," he replied, turning back to the paddock. Steam plumed from the mare's mouth as she daintily took the dried grass from J.J.'s hand.

Winter was cold but simple on a ranch—keep an eye on the cattle and horses, feed them the hay stored in the big barn, wait for spring. April should have been here....

He shied from the thought and the memories that cut fresh and deep at this moment, brought on by the strange visit from Sissy.

Dawn touched his arm in the warm, sympathetic way she had. She was his best friend—a fact his half brother accepted, but not without a twinge of jealous wariness.

"Over what?" she asked.

He debated telling her, but the need to talk overran the instinct to ignore Sissy and her ridiculous accusation or whatever the hell it was.

"Sissy was here this morning."

"Sissy? Oh, Celia Campbell. Was that who it was? I saw the car leave, but couldn't see the driver. Was she looking for me? We're supposed to plan an Easter program for the folks at the senior citizens' home for next month."

"No, she wanted me." He laughed harshly at the irony in that statement.

"Oh?" Dawn gave him a curious perusal.

"She's pregnant," he said, not knowing how to pretty it up. "She says it's mine."

"*Oh,*" Dawn said again, only this time it was with shock and disbelief rolled into the word. "Is... Could it..." She cleared her throat. "Do you want to talk about it?"

"It's not mine." He gripped the railing savagely. "I'd have remembered—" He broke off as an odd sensation rolled through him, one he couldn't identify. Those hands stroking over him... No, that was imagination, not memory.

His sister-in-law looked more and more puzzled. "You don't remember? Not at all?"

Her voice trailed off in stunned amazement.

He felt heat sweep up his neck. His ears were probably glowing. He shook his head.

"When did this supposedly happen?"

"New Year's Eve."

She nodded and gave him a sympathetic glance. "Jackson and I were worried about you that night. You'd been remote and irritable all week. I called to invite you to have dinner with us, but you weren't home. Your mother said you'd gone to the country club for dinner and the dance."

"Yeah. I went for some stupid reason that I don't remember. In fact, I can't remember much about that night. I don't recall leaving the club or driving home. The one thing I do remember was waking up the next morning with a hell of a hangover."

The last thing he'd wanted to watch that night was the marital bliss of Dawn and Jackson. That was what had driven him from the ranch—that and the silence.

April's laughter. That was what he missed the most. Her laughter and her teasing ways. Ah, God...

Hunter studied the horizon where a few storm clouds were collecting. He was aware of Dawn's gaze, her eyes the same light blue her sister's had been.

"Celia isn't a liar," Dawn said thoughtfully, more as if she was trying to figure this out than converse with him. "I can't imagine her saying something this serious if it wasn't true. I mean, I don't think she has enough guile to pull something like this off."

He intercepted her apologetic glance with a hard one of his own. "You think I could have made love to a woman, even an airhead like Sissy, and not remember?''

Dawn's frown was a reprimand. "She prefers to be called Celia, and she isn't an airhead. She's just unsure of herself. I've heard good things about her since she returned here to live. She got a job as a teacher's aide in the kindergarten classes. You should see her with the people at the nursing home. She's good with them, and smart, too—"

"Trying to trap a man into marriage with the oldest trick in the book isn't very smart." He was gratified at Dawn's gasp.

"She demanded marriage?" she asked incredulously. "I can't believe it. No sane woman would do such a thing, not without being sure she knew exactly what she was talking about."

He tried to recall the conversation. "She didn't mention marriage," he conceded.

"What did she say?"

"That, well, she was pregnant." He felt his ears go warm again. "She said New Year's Day was her birthday and she was thirty. She'd planned on having two children by then. She thanked me for giving her the birthday present—"

He broke off when Dawn made a choking sound and covered her mouth with one hand, shaking her head as she did.

"What?" he snapped.

His sister-in-law composed herself with an effort. "That is so like Celia. Thanking you for doing her a favor. As if you got nothing from it." She pressed her lips tightly together and said nothing more.

Hunter had the feeling Dawn would burst out

laughing if he so much as looked at her cross-eyed. He felt like pounding something into the dirt. "Where's Jackson?" he asked. "We were supposed to work with the colts today."

"Oh, no, you're not going to start a fight and take your frustrations out on him. You need to talk this out with Celia. She wouldn't say she was expecting your child if she didn't have good reason to think it is yours. If you truly can't remember, then who's to say it isn't?"

"Me. I say it isn't." He spun away from her watchful gaze. "I haven't been able to make love to a woman—any woman—since April. I've tried. After you and Jackson married, I dated a couple of women in Reno I knew from college days. Neither worked out. They were attractive, but I didn't...react."

His son, walking along the fence, the dog at his heels, glanced back at him with his big blue eyes. April's eyes. Hunter looked away. Sometimes he felt his son's reproach, as if somehow he should have prevented April's death.

Driving cattle to market was a normal ranch chore. On that fateful day, a swarm of bees had startled the critters, making them panic. The stupid animals had tried to climb out of the truck. The vehicle had tilted, then rolled over an embankment, killing April and her father instantly. Even if Hunter had been right behind them, he couldn't have saved either of them.

He'd been the one to find the truck. Lifting April's lifeless form from the ditch had been the hardest thing he'd ever done. Her white-blond hair had been matted with blood and dirt. Her skin, as pale as moonlight, had been mottled with bruises. He'd cursed the fate that had done this to his beautiful, his perfect love.

The pain hit him as it always did when he thought of that day. Ah, God…

Dawn nodded wisely. "The sickness of the heart. That's what Jackson's Aunt Maggie would call it. Only you can overcome it. Celia hasn't had it easy, either. Remember when your aunt ran off with Celia's father? She cried, Hunter. We were at a drill-team camp. She slipped away. I found her sobbing her heart out. She was sixteen."

"Yeah, life is tough," he mocked.

Dawn gripped his arm. "Maybe with Celia you can find a new life. Oh, Hunter, wouldn't that be wonderful? A new life and a new love—"

He shook off the notion savagely. "Don't be crazy. I'm not in love with Sissy…Celia Campbell."

"Don't be too hard on her. I'm sure there's some explanation. Maybe you'd better talk to her when you calm down and are able to think rationally about this."

"I am rational. She's the one who's hallucinating. I would never do to my son what my father did to me."

"Sire an illegitimate child," she said softly, glancing toward the house his half-brother, Jackson, had built when he'd moved to the ranch.

It had been a shock when Hunter's father's will had been read and he'd found out there was another son. His trust in the one person he'd thought was right up there with the saints when it came to integrity had been badly shaken. Hunter would never do such a thing to his son.

But what if there was a kid? And Sis—Celia went around telling people it was his?

"You're right. I will talk to her. I'll get to the bottom of this if it's the last thing I do."

Chapter Two

"**Y**ou're what?"

Really, Celia was getting a little upset with people looking at her as if she'd lost her mind when she made her big announcement. "Expecting, Mother. A child."

"I didn't think you were expecting the Easter bunny," her mother snapped. "I suppose you're going to get married."

The idea was obviously repugnant to Mrs. Campbell, but then Celia knew her mom didn't like men or marriage.

"Well, no. Not exactly." She wondered why she'd added the qualifier. *Not at all* was the appropriate answer. "I decided I wanted a child. I don't need a husband."

"Good. That's the first sensible thing you've said this evening. So you felt the call of nature, did you?"

Celia glanced at her mother uneasily, not sure what she meant. When she'd phoned to break the news, her mom had invited her to dinner. She'd decided to drive to Reno and announce the coming birth in person.

Why did she always feel compelled to do things the hard way? She sighed. It was a trait of hers, and her night with Hunter McLean was a prime example of it in action.

She should have gone to a sperm bank. Then she'd have none of this guilt eating at her. However, it wasn't as if she'd taken advantage of him. She'd asked. He'd said yes. It should have been simple.

Except nothing in life ever was.

"'Nature'?" Celia repeated, feeling flutters of anxiety rush through her. She wasn't going to discuss her libido with anyone, especially her mother.

"The biological clock ticking. You just turned thirty. You're on the downhill slide. Lots of single women start to feel the first twinges of desperation."

"I'm hardly desperate. I simply wanted a child. It's something I've planned for all my life. I want this child," she said for emphasis, recalling her youth and the pain of knowing she was the cause of her parents' bondage.

"So when are you due?"

"The end of September. I conceived on New Year's," she said. Images immediately poured into her mind. She'd never forget that night.

Her mother lit one of the five low-tar-and-nicotine cigarettes she allowed herself each day.

The scent of the smoke hit Celia's nostrils. With a groan, she rushed for the bathroom and splashed water on her face until the queasiness passed. When she returned, she picked up her purse and jacket.

"I think I'll go home."

"Tomorrow is Sunday. Stay the night."

"The drive is easy." She crept toward the door. She always found it hard to follow her inclinations when someone ordered her to do something else.

"You always preferred that cabin to a real house," her mother remarked, walking her to the door.

"Well, Gran gave it to me. I loved visiting her and grandfather there in the summers. I remember when all of us—you and Father and I—lived at Honey Lake, then later, when you and I went there for long weekends—"

"I hated it. Nothing to do but hike and fish. How do you keep busy all year?"

"Well, there's the nursing home. Dawn McLean and I lead exercises there twice a week. I work at the school for four hours each morning. Several of us have dinner together every Friday at the restaurant on the lake. The town is friendly. Everyone knows everyone."

"And everyone's business. It was horrible when your father left. Everyone knew, probably before I did."

Celia flinched at the bitterness in her mother's tone. Fourteen years and she still hadn't forgiven her husband for embarrassing her like that. But Celia knew it had hurt, too. She touched her mother's shoulder sympathetically.

"I really should be going. Thanks for a wonderful dinner. It was lovely talking to you."

"Be careful on the drive. By the way, who is the father of your child? Do you know?"

Celia felt the blush all the way to her scalp. "Of course. I was very careful in selecting the gene pool."

She had thought it all out since seeing Hunter yesterday and could honestly say this. Although the actual act had been a bit impulsive—a thing of the moment, so to speak—still, upon consideration, she knew that she would never have chosen anyone but him.

"It was Hunter McLean."

"My God. It was his aunt that ran off with your father."

"Yes, I know, but I didn't think it would matter. I mean, he does have good bloodlines."

Her mother's lips curled sardonically as she gave a last warning. "Whatever you do, don't marry him."

Celia thought of her mother's parting advice as she supervised the five-year-olds in the playground.

Marriage? No chance of that. Hunter had made it clear he didn't want her—that is, marriage to her, or anything like that. Not that she'd expected it. She doubted he ever wanted to set eyes on her again, judging by his expression when she fled his house.

She spread her hand over her as-yet-flat tummy. "I want you," she whispered fiercely to her child.

"Talking to yourself?" Terri, the kindergarten teacher, came outside and took a seat on the bench in the warm sun.

"Sort of."

Spring was in the air—a bit early, but Celia could feel it. It was as if the life stirring from its winter sleep deep in the earth reached right up through the soles of her shoes and joined the life growing within her.

She sat beside her friend, her eyes on the shouting, playing kids. "Raymundo, no running, please."

"Sorry," the boy called. "Look, I'm skipping, Miss Campbell. See? I'm skipping."

She nodded to him before glancing at Terri. "I have some news. You might be shocked."

Terri's brown eyes opened wide. "Tell me more."

"I'm going to have a baby."

"A baby?"

"At least you didn't say *A what?* in shocked tones like others I could name," she replied with a laugh. She checked over the playground to see that everyone was behaving.

"The father, I assume?" Terri inquired.

She realized, given Hunter's attitude, she couldn't disclose him as the father. "My mother. I told her over the weekend."

"What did she say?"

Celia managed a laugh. "Don't get married."

Terri rolled her eyes. "And the father?"

"Well, that's a little trickier."

"Are you going to tell me who?"

"I can't. It was a sperm donor." She told the lie without blushing. Basically, that was all Hunter had been, so that was the end of it.

Terri made a strangled sound and stared at Celia as if she'd grown two heads. "You didn't."

"Yes. Why not?"

Her friend shook her head. "The school board won't allow it."

"I beg your pardon?"

"Celia, this isn't Reno. It's a ranching community. Church and Little League and the Rotary Club. I don't think they'll welcome an unwed mom working with their sweet wee ones with open arms and great heaps of understanding."

She hadn't thought of that. "I have to work. I don't have enough money to stay at home full-time."

Terri gave her a sympathetic pat on the shoulder. "Then I suggest you contact the father and arrange a quick marriage."

"I told you there wasn't—" Celia stopped. "You don't believe me."

Terri shook her head. She gave Celia a sympathetic glance and smiled encouragingly. "If you've had a quarrel, make it up. You can always divorce him after the baby is born."

Celia gasped.

The teacher laughed. "Just joking. But you'd better figure out something, and fast. When you start showing, the town fathers, bless their pea-size minds, will start asking questions. You'd better have answers."

"I guess I can't say I recently got divorced from some fictional husband in Reno and didn't realize at the time I was pregnant?"

"Well, you could, but I haven't seen you with a man since you came back here to live a year ago. Who's going to believe a mysterious husband who's never been seen? Are you going to tell the gang at dinner tonight?"

Celia shook her head. "Maybe I'd better think about what I'm going to do. If worse came to worst, I suppose I could move back to Reno and ask my mom if she'd let me live with her while I finish getting my teaching degree. I wish I didn't have two whole years to go on it.''

''I hate to see you have to pull up roots again. You've been happy here, haven't you?''

Celia nodded, her thoughts on the future and its problems suddenly leering at her. There might be catastrophes out there that she hadn't even considered.

And Hunter. What would he do?

''This is looking tougher than I thought,'' she murmured. She laid a hand over her tummy. ''But no one is going to hurt this baby. I'll see to that.''

''How?''

''I can sell the homestead here, then move someplace where no one knows me. I'll tell everyone I'm a widow and that my husband was a rancher who got kicked in the head by a mad cow and died instantly.''

Terri stared at her in amazement.

Celia grinned self-consciously. Then they started laughing at the whole ridiculous situation.

When it was time to go in, Celia blew the whistle. The kids all lined up. She looked at their flushed, happy faces, and her heart clenched. Children should only find love waiting for them when they came into the world.

Celia pulled into her drive at 9:42 that evening. She hit the brakes to keep from running into a black pickup truck that was all but invisible in the darkness under the fir trees that lined the drive.

Heart thudding from the near mishap, she edged around the truck and punched the garage-door opener. The outside light came on. It disclosed a male figure sitting on the steps at the side entrance to her home. He stood as she swept by.

She didn't need the light to know who the brawny male was. Hunter McLean, wearing a thick sheepskin jacket, cast a formidable shadow across the lawn.

In college, she'd attended a biofeedback seminar where she'd learned deep breathing as an antidote to panic. She tried it now before climbing out of her car and facing Hunter again. She'd hardly drawn one breath before he jerked the car door open.

"We need to talk," he informed her in a low, gruff voice that chilled her like a northern gale.

"Well, okay."

Bright, really bright, she reprimanded herself as she led the way inside her snug home. She should send him packing and tell him to call for an appointment if he wanted to see her. She didn't, though. She couldn't be that rude—even to Hunter, who probably deserved it.

She stuck her purse in the drawer where she kept it, hung up her coat and kicked off her boots. Her feet were swollen and aching. Her tummy was queasy.

Morning sickness? Ha! Try morning, noon and night.

"Here, let me take your jacket," she said. "Would you like some coffee?"

"Yes."

"Decaffeinated okay?"

"Yes."

He watched her, like a fox spying out the chicken coop, while she did the mundane tasks. When the coffee was brewing, she opened a cake canister. The rich, fruity scent of pineapple cake hit her nostrils and went straight to her stomach. "Excuse me."

She headed for the master bathroom at a run. When she stopped retching, she splashed water on her face, then brushed her teeth. Staring at her reflection in the mirror, she noted the bloodshot eyes, the wet strands of hair sticking to her temples and the side of her neck.

Well, she'd looked worse. And there had been times when she'd looked better. She sighed.

After smoothing on a pink lip gloss, she felt ready to face Hunter again. As ready as she'd ever be to get her head snapped off, she decided with fatalistic humor.

When she opened the door, Hunter stood on the other side, leaning against her bedroom wall. She nearly jumped out of her skin.

"You scared me," she accused. "Don't ever do that again."

"Yes, ma'am," he drawled. His expression softened fractionally. "I wanted to make sure you were all right."

"Yes, I am." She was so irritated, she wanted to slap him. She might have if he hadn't been twice her size.

"April was grouchy during her pregnancy, too," he said, following her to the dresser where she removed her earrings and necklace. A flash of emotion appeared in his eyes and was gone.

"I'm sorry," she said.

"For what?"

"For reminding you of her."

Celia knew how it felt to lose a loved one. When

her father had left, a hole had opened inside her. She'd thought it was her fault; that if she'd behaved better, studied harder, or something, he would have stayed. It had taken a long time to realize she had nothing to do with his leaving.

She saw Hunter's gaze flick to the standard-size bed. He had been too tall for it. His feet had dangled off the end. They'd laughed. Then he'd kissed her... and kissed her...and kissed her.

His touch had been so exquisitely gentle, this brawny bear of a man. He'd cupped her breasts—first one, then the other—and had kissed them, too.

"Perfect," he'd murmured, circling his tongue over their engorged tips.

She'd have loved him for that alone since she'd always been sensitive about her appearance. He had assured her she was beautiful. He'd said her skin was like ambrosia. He had paid her a host of other compliments that night.

Of course, she'd known they were all lies, but she'd been enchanted by his sweet murmurings and had fallen a bit in love with him at each one.

When he'd finally come to her, after waiting until her nervousness disappeared completely under the onslaught of his caresses, he had been wonderful. He'd known what to say, how to touch, when to move on.

She'd finally found the magic of lovemaking—the heat, the panting excitement, the explosive release into bliss.... She wished he'd do it again.

Her thoughts scattered to the four winds when Hunter gestured toward the bed. "Is this where it happened?"

He made it sound as if a criminal act had been perpetrated on the spot.

"Where my child was conceived, yes." She lifted her chin, daring him to say something derisive.

"And mine, according to you." His gaze cut into her as if it were a laser beam directed at her soul.

She turned back to the mirror and fussed with her hair, fluffing the damp tendrils away from her face. "I didn't dream your presence that night."

His chest lifted. He let the breath go in a rush. "I'm not going to sire a bastard," he said ominously.

That sounded as if it could be another of those trick remarks he was so good at throwing around. She tried to figure it out, but her head was pounding.

So was her heart. She was increasingly aware of him and that they were in her bedroom. He'd undressed her in here.

She'd watched, fascinated, while he'd done the same for himself. Each part of him had been beautiful.

He'd made her feel beautiful, too. Beautiful and desirable. He had wanted her. She certainly hadn't imagined that. Desire was something he couldn't hide.

"Have you remembered?" she asked hopefully.

"No."

"Oh." She stared at him, puzzled. "I read that men couldn't, uh, well, that alcohol interfered with... But you couldn't have been drunk. We had cocoa and talked for an hour, then it was midnight and we kissed. After that, we... You... Everything worked fine...."

His snort of sardonic laughter shut her up.

''The coffee should be ready,'' she said inanely and rushed from the bedroom.

The house, meant to be a summer home although her grandparents had decided to live here year-round, had only two bedrooms, each with its own bathroom, a high-ceilinged living room, a tiny study and a kitchen, which also served as the dining room.

It was plain and homey, and she loved it. It had been her refuge in the summers after she and her mother had moved to Reno. With Hunter on the premises, she felt invaded.

He stayed right behind her until they returned to the kitchen as if he thought she might break and run for cover at any second. He took a seat at the round oak table that had belonged to Gran's grandmother.

Celia poured coffee and cut wedges from the pineapple cake she'd baked to take to the nursing home the next day.

Hunter was silent, his eyes dark green and thoughtful, while she served them and laid out napkins and forks on opposite sides of the table.

A sigh forced its way from her throat when she joined him. She realized she was terribly weary. ''It's ten,'' she announced, hoping this would make him eat up and go.

He took a bite of cake and looked mildly surprised. ''This is good. Did you make it?''

''With a little help from Betty Crocker,'' she told him. ''You probably didn't mean it that way, but it really is insulting to imply another isn't skilled at something.'' She was tired of his skepticism toward her.

He hadn't been that way when they'd made love.

He'd been sweet and funny and cherishing and, oh, so many other wonderful things. It was difficult to believe this was the same man. She could have fallen in love with that other Hunter—the gentle caring one.

Maybe she had dreamed that night. The man who'd shared her bed hadn't been anything like this scowling, tough-minded rancher. Except that she was carrying his child, it was as if those moments had never been.

"Sorry. I've never found myself in this situation before. It's a little hard to swallow."

"Try gingko," she suggested. "That's supposed to be good for the memory. It improves the circulation."

She paused when he lifted his head and stared at her as if she were from another planet.

"Dawn can tell you. She knows all about herbs." Celia patted her mouth with the napkin when he continued to watch her. He could make her quake with just a glance.

Hunter finished his cake and pushed the plate aside. Leaning back in the chair, both hands cupped around the coffee mug, he asked, "You swear the child is mine? There's no chance of it being someone else's?"

"Yes. I swear. I mean, of course it couldn't be anyone else's. I haven't been—"

"With another man for five years," he finished for her. He thumped the heel of his hand on the table in frustration. "I wish I knew what to believe."

She practiced deep breathing until the spasm of pain passed, and with it, the anger.

He didn't believe her. He would never believe her.

So, who needed him to? She wasn't asking anything from him. "I'd like to go to bed now, Hunter—"

His head jerked up. He stared at her with the coldest gaze she'd ever seen.

"Alone," she added. "It's been a long week."

"I'll bet."

She watched the steam rising from the coffee and didn't bother with an answer.

"Make me see that night," he finally continued. "Give me some proof that what you said really happened."

She stared at him, aghast. "How? Do you want me to give you a blow-by-blow account of the evening?"

"Yes."

"All right." She let herself remember the night. "I went to the country club at Terri's insistence. She and her husband picked me up. She's the kindergarten teacher—"

"I know who she is," he interrupted impatiently.

"Of course. You sat at the same table at dinner, then we went into the ballroom together. We shared a bottle of champagne. After a couple of dances, you disappeared. I saw you at the bar later."

"Yeah, I remember some of that."

"You said you were leaving. Adam came up. He said you shouldn't drive and grabbed your keys. You objected. I was afraid you were going to fight, so I volunteered to drive you home. You agreed." She paused to let that sink in.

"I agreed to let a woman drive me home on a subzero night with ice on the road? I must have been looped."

"That's what you said when we got on the road.

You wanted to stop at the diner and have some coffee instead. I offered to make it at my house. So that's what we did."

"And once we got there, one thing led to another...." He let the thought trail off.

She had to be completely truthful. "I was out of regular coffee, so I made cocoa instead. We sat in front of the fire and talked until midnight."

"About what?"

He evidently couldn't imagine what they might have in common to discuss. She wasn't going to tell him of the loneliness he'd talked about and the emptiness of his life. She wasn't going to mention the secrets of her soul that she'd bared to him that night along with the secrets of her body.

"Just...things. Then midnight came and we realized what time it was. We kissed. It seemed natural. I mean, everyone does. Then the kiss changed and..." She couldn't say the words.

"And we proceeded from there?"

She nodded.

"Did I carry you to the bedroom?" he asked softly, his eyes narrowed as he studied her. "Did I undress you? Or did you undress me?"

She shook her head, refusing to answer, aware that he was mocking her as she tried to help him recall the night.

"A little of both, huh?"

He moved closer, and she felt his heat like that from a stove radiating over her. The same wild yearning to touch him overcame her survival instincts. She laid her hands on his chest.

Grabbing her wrists, he leaned down to her, his

breath fanning gently over her forehead. "Maybe I should ask Adam if his memories of that night jibe with yours."

Anger, as pure and clear and sharp as mountain air, rolled through her at his continued doubt. For a heartbeat, she felt she could hate him.

"You don't have to," she said, trying to look defeated and dejected. "I lied. I wanted to trap you into marriage, just as you said. I see it won't work."

His eyes narrowed to glittering slits. "Was there any truth in what you've told me?"

"No."

He gave her a little shake. "Is that the truth?"

"Yes," she said, now trying for open and honest. "I'm not expecting at all. I thought if we married and I got pregnant right away, you might never know."

A shocked silence followed her statement.

"The sickness—"

"I faked it. Now would you please go? I'd really like to get some rest," she finished.

For a moment, she thought he was going to refuse, then he released her, jammed his hat on his head, retrieved his coat and left without another word.

Chapter Three

The buzz was loud in the teachers' lounge when Celia arrived, swept in on a bitter cold wind that heralded snow before the day was out.

"Did you hear the latest?" Sheila, the sixth-grade teacher, asked.

Celia laid her purse on the rickety table where Sheila, Terri and the other kindergarten teacher sat.

"What's that?" she asked, stifling a yawn.

She hadn't slept well over the weekend. The morning-noon-and-night sickness had been particularly virulent. The doctor had given her medicine for it, but it didn't seem to have helped at all.

"The high-school history teacher and the assistant coach were caught in the parking lot after the basketball game Friday night," Sheila related the gossip in a low voice. "It looks as if they've been carrying on for ages."

"'Carrying on'?" Celia repeated, her brain befuddled with her own problems.

"Yeah. As in flagrante delicto. The principal had stayed late after the game, talking to the guard about the break-in they'd had last week. When he left, he saw the car parked in the shadows behind the gym and went to check it out, figuring it was teenagers up to mischief."

"But it wasn't," Terri said, giving Celia a significant glance that caused an added chill to race up her spine.

She hung her coat in her locker, then poured a cup of coffee and sipped experimentally, giving her stomach a chance to accept the hot brew rather than spew it right back. She wondered if she could hold out for the month or two it supposedly took to get over this dratted queasiness. She took a seat at the table.

"What happened?" she asked, curious yet dreading the answer.

Sheila leaned close and spoke in a whisper. "I understand they were in the backseat. They didn't even have the doors locked."

The hair rose on Celia's neck.

"When Mr. Waters jerked the door open and found two of his teachers…" Sheila's voice trailed off, and she paused, her eyebrows disappearing under her bangs. "The old buzzard nearly had a heart attack."

"I can imagine," Celia murmured, torn between sympathy for the couple and disapproval for their "carrying on" in general and at that location in particular.

"No, no, really. He grabbed his chest and gasped, in moral outrage, one can only assume, then collapsed on top of them. The guard, seeing the lights come on in the car, came over to see what was going on—'' Sheila broke into a giggle and stopped for a second before she was able to continue.

Celia could tell the situation was going to deteriorate rapidly. Her sympathy was won by the couple.

"It isn't funny, but, my gosh, what a farce. The guard couldn't figure out what was going on. He thought Mr. Waters was being attacked by a gargoyle or something. He started beating off the coach, who was trying to do CPR on the principal. The history teacher was scrabbling about and jerking clothes on—'' Sheila covered her mouth with both hands and shook her head, unable to continue.

"And things got worse from there," Terri said, giving Celia another penetrating glance. "They took Mr. Waters to the hospital. He was diagnosed with heart palpitations."

The other kindergarten teacher spoke up. "My grandmother had heart palpitations. I thought that was something old ladies got when they were shocked."

"And old men," Terri amended with a wry grin.

"I think it means the heartbeats go erratic," Celia said. "He's all right?"

"Oh, yes," Sheila said. "They gave him a tranquillizer and sent him home. He was fine Saturday morning."

"Yeah, he went straight to the superintendent. Both teachers have been suspended without pay while the school board decides what to do." Terri gave Celia a nudge under the table with her foot.

"They'll lose their jobs," Sheila predicted. "Don't you remember? That's what happened to the junior-high science teacher and the school nurse when they were caught kissing in the clinic two years ago.''

"But she's back now," Celia reminded them.

"Yeah, because they couldn't find another nurse who would work for slave wages," Terri remarked, giving her a third warning glance.

Celia didn't need the pointed reminders of her own predicament. She could see the writing on the wall without help from her friend. She'd be fired, too, and the principal wouldn't have any problem whatsoever replacing her.

What had she gotten herself into with that impulsive act on New Year's Eve?

Depression dampened the joy she usually felt when she thought of her child. She wouldn't let it be the subject of gossip and ridicule. She knew the pain of that, of holding her head high and pretending everyone wasn't talking about her father and the teacher he'd been carrying on with before telling her mother he wanted a divorce.

She sighed as gloom settled over her. Looking out the window, she saw the first snowflakes begin to fall.

Hunter eyed the trunk at the end of the bed and the suitcase lying open on the bed. "Sure you have enough clothes?" he asked with an ironic inflection.

His mother stopped sorting blouses and looked up with an absentminded frown. "Do you think I should take another suitcase? The girl at the travel office said to dress in layers for changes in the weather.''

Hunter hid a smile and winked at his son, who was playing with an airplane he'd fashioned from building blocks. J.J. gave him a solemn glance, then went back to his playing.

"I guess if I were going on a six-month cruise, I'd take everything I own. For me, one suitcase should handle that with enough extra room to pack my horse and saddle."

Margaret McLean removed a red silk blouse from its hanger and rolled it with tissue in the middle. She tucked it neatly into the case. "There, that gives me a week's worth of clothing in case the trunk gets lost."

"Mom, the trunk will be on the ship with you."

"Yes, but we have to fly to Miami first, then a van is supposed to pick us up, then they have to sort the luggage and get it to our suite— Oh, you're teasing me," she said, finally focusing her full attention on him.

"Yeah." He eyed the piles of clothing. "I can't imagine you leaving the ranch for six months."

She dropped her hands to the arms of her wheelchair and turned it so she could face him. "It's something I've always wanted to do, but your father could never tear himself away from here long enough to go on a two-week vacation, much less an extended one. Like him, you think the sun rises and sets on this piece of land. It doesn't."

Her statement took him by surprise. She sounded almost bitter about it, and he would have sworn she loved the ranch as much as his father had.

"You'll need to get someone in to take care of J.J. when you're not available. You can't expect Dawn and Hazel to do it for you. You also need a housekeeper. You can handle the ranch, but you can't keep up with the housework at the same time.''

"What happened to the woman you hired last month?"

"She said it was too much work."

"Huh. You and Anna handled it all for years, and you were in the wheelchair most of that time."

"Women don't want to slave for men anymore." His mother gave him a calculating glance. "I suggest you marry some naive young thing who thinks you're wonderful. Actually, you need a ranch girl who knows how to work. Better yet, find someone who fits both descriptions."

Hunter shifted uneasily from one leg to the other. He'd never heard his mother use that particularly dry, stinging tone before. Since his bastard brother had come to the ranch to claim his half of their father's inheritance, Hunter had known his mother was restless and resentful of that fact, but he hadn't realized the depth of her dissatisfaction with ranch life until now.

He hitched his thumbs in his back pockets, his mind on the future. He didn't like things changing for no good reason—

A child was no good reason?

He frowned sharply, as if the question had been asked by an outsider rather than coming from some deep place inside him. Looking at his son busy at his quiet play, Hunter felt a hard, painful clenching in his chest.

It was March 14, two weeks since Sissy—Celia, as she insisted—had come to him with her news. He was no nearer to figuring out that scene, or the one at her house, than he'd been at the time. However, he'd heard no more from her, so he figured she'd given up her pursuit.

"Marriage?" He snorted to show what he thought of that idea. He wanted no part of that god-awful aching need that came with loving another person. Never again.

Not that he'd fall in love with an airhead like Celia Campbell. She must have been out of her mind when she'd thought of pulling her little stunt.

He realized his mother was looking at him, with more than a little exasperation in her expression. "Sorry, what did you say?"

"J.J. needs a mother." She delivered it as a blunt statement of fact, one that implied he should see it for himself.

Anger curled in him. Everyone seemed to know what he ought to be doing. Everyone but him. Hell, Dawn had thought marriage was a great idea, too.

"There's more that comes into it than that," he said stiffly. "I'm not interested in marrying again."

His failures in that regard rose like a haunting vapor in him. A damn poor husband he'd make for a woman when he couldn't touch one without that black hole opening up inside him like a toothache.

He had a sudden picture of hands—small hands with short, rosy nails and skin that still showed traces of last year's tan. He frowned, puzzled. How had he known that?

The image remained, and with it, the tactile sensation of being touched. He could feel those hands gliding down his sides and onto his thighs, then touching him in the most intimate way....

Heat ran rampant through him. He almost groaned aloud, but managed to bite it back. There was within him something that was stronger than a dream, but not as defined as a memory. It was driving him insane.

"Your father made the ultimate sacrifice for the ranch by marrying me and getting a loan from my father so he could make it through a bad spot. Would you do less?"

"I don't know. The situation never came up." The words came out rougher than he'd intended.

His son stopped skimming his homebuilt airplane along the carpet and stared up at him. The child's eyes were the pale blue of the morning sky and seemed to look right inside him to his soul—or where his soul used to be. Now there was simply an empty spot that was sometimes painful, the way he'd heard a severed limb would ache.

The phone rang. His mother answered, listened, thanked the caller, then hung up.

"That was Adam. He says the medicine is ready to be picked up."

He nodded. "I'd better run in and get it." He turned to J.J. "Come on, old son, we have work to do."

"Let him stay with me," his mother requested. "I'll fix supper for us. Tom's cooking for the hands tonight. You can eat in town if you'd like."

Hunter bent to his son. "I need to go to town. Would you like to go, or do you want to stay here with your grandmother?"

The blue eyes met his, then looked down. J.J. pointed to his grandmother. Hunter sighed as something akin to despair settled into the hole that used to be his soul.

"Okay then," he announced with false heartiness. "Maybe Adam will have time for dinner." He tousled J.J.'s dark hair before leaving his mother and son in the bedroom that used to be a study before the auto accident that had put her in a wheelchair for the rest of her life.

He shook his head as he backed the pickup out of the drive a few minutes later. He had been feeling morbid this last week. Off his feed, too. He hadn't eaten much in days. A steak at the restaurant by the lake sounded good.

Hunter folded the receipt and stuck his checkbook inside the inner pocket of his jacket. He watched the snow falling while he waited for Adam to finish with his last patient.

He had a sense of time passing, of being left behind, but he didn't know what was running off and leaving him.

Except his mother, of course.

Maybe things would lighten up around the house with her gone. He'd spend more time with J.J. and less on chores. He'd let the four ranch hands they hired each spring take over the work. Jackson could oversee the ranch as well as he could, although his half brother liked working with the horses and supervising the logging operations rather than dealing with cattle.

Tough. He had to fill in where he was needed. Dawn and her mother, Hazel Ericson, would help with J.J. With two grandmothers and an aunt always around, he'd never had to worry about having a baby-sitter handy for the boy. With his mother leaving—and he had a feeling she wouldn't return to the ranch—that was about to change.

Her advice jangled in his mind like a discordant note played over and over. A sweet young thing? Naive?

Celia, in her miniskirt and boots, her body curvy and supple, her smile bright, came to mind.

He shook his head slightly. She was neither sweet nor all that young. Thirty. Three years younger than he was, although she'd only been two years behind him in school.

Maybe she was smarter than he gave her credit for. One thing for sure, she had him in a quandary.

"Hey, old son, why the long face?" Adam emerged from the back of the veterinarian's office. "Did the cow die before the medicine came in?"

Since he asked this last quite cheerfully, Hunter smiled sardonically. "Nope. She's out in the barn, bellowing up a storm."

"Ah, so she's what brought on this latest blizzard. I should encourage you to go home and give her the medicine as fast as possible, huh?"

"After dinner. I want to talk to you."

Adam gave him a sharp glance at his serious tone. "Okay. I'll meet you at the restaurant."

Hunter nodded and headed out into the snow. The flakes hit his face with stinging force, turning his nose red and making his eyes water. It was a bitter storm, the snow wet and heavy and dangerous. He'd better not stay out late or the country roads would be impassable until the snowplow came through.

After parking in the lot across the street, Hunter ducked his head and raced for the door of the popular local spot with its view of Honey Lake. Adam, a step ahead of him, broke into a run, too, beating him by a split second. Hunter returned his friend's grin, realizing they'd fallen into their old schoolboy habit of trying to beat out each other.

The scent of ribs slow roasting over hot coals tempted his appetite once they were inside. The place was busy, but they were seated at a table by the front window at once.

"Ribs," Adam said. "Plenty of fries on the side. Slaw. Beer. Whatever you have on tap."

"Same here," Hunter echoed.

The waitress set their water down and grabbed her pad. She frowned as she wrote the order, then flounced off with the menus still under her arm.

"You'd think by now she'd know we always order the same thing," Adam remarked, watching the sway of her rear end in the tight jeans with amused appreciation.

"Yeah."

The waitress returned with the brimming beer mugs, slapped them on the table and went to greet the next customers stamping snow off their shoes at the door.

"Here's to you." Adam lifted the mug.

Hunter clicked the thick, frosty glass against the vet's, then took a deep drink. "Ah," he said. "There's nothing like that first gulp to quench a man's thirst."

Adam, still concentrating on the waitress, smiled. "Depends on what kind of thirst you've got."

"Hey, your wife out of town?"

"Naw. My mother-in-law is visiting. She stays up until two o'clock in the morning, watching old movies on television." Adam yawned, then grimaced. "The wife stays up with her, and they're both still sleeping when I leave in the morning. The kid has breakfast with me and gets herself off to school."

"Janie must be nearly grown by now."

"Thirteen, going on thirty. She told me she had a crush on some kid at school, but when he started liking her, she didn't like him anymore. She wanted to know why. She was worried she was fickle. Her best friend has liked the same boy all year." Adam huffed a sigh. "Man, kids are tough."

"Yeah," Hunter agreed, his worry over J.J. surfacing. "The doctors over at the clinic think I should send J.J. to some special school in San Francisco. I don't know."

"Like a boarding school?"

"Yeah."

"He's too young," Adam declared, as convincing as the experts had been in their opinion. "Keep him at home until he's old enough to understand why he's being sent off. When my parents sent me off to camp when I was five, I thought they'd put me in some kind of Outward Bound orphanage. I didn't believe my mom when she said they'd be back."

"Damn," Hunter murmured.

"Yeah, it was pretty awful, although I admit, after I got over being abandoned, I had a pretty good time."

Hunter grinned at the wry tone, then became somber. Another group came into the restaurant—three women, laughing and chattering in their tinkling voices. He watched them settle, moodiness dropping over him.

"Hey, man, you here?"

He glanced at Adam and took another draft of beer. "Tell me something. Did you take my keys at the country club on New Year's Eve?"

Adam was plainly surprised by the question. "Yeah. I thought you shouldn't drive. I offered to take you home, but you weren't having any of it."

"So then Sis—Celia Campbell came to my rescue?"

"Or mine," Adam said and chuckled. "You seemed inclined to fight about it until she stepped in. She said she was without wheels and was ready to go home, that you'd be doing her a favor if she could get a lift."

"Hmm." Hunter frowned as he tried to bring the related happening to mind. He couldn't. The Scotch he'd guzzled after he'd gotten home must have blotted out the incidents prior to that. "So I left with her?"

"Right." Adam peered at him, puzzled, then his face cleared as he figured it out. "Ah, you don't remember, do you? See? You were three sheets to the wind and listing heavily, just like I told you when you were arguing you could drive with one hand tied behind your back."

Hunter's stomach dropped forty stories on an imaginary elevator. He suddenly saw himself standing at the country club's old-fashioned Western bar, arrogantly telling Adam he was in fine shape to drive while he held on to the bar to stop the strange swaying of the room.

The next image was stranger still. He had his arm around a woman's shoulders. She was a small person, and she smelled good. He remembered that. She led him out of the cold and into some warm place....

Hearing a woman's laughter, his stomach lurched again. He jerked around. The three women had been seated near them. They were still talking and laughing the way women always did, as if they had ten topics to discuss and only a few minutes to cover them.

Their meal arrived. For some reason, the spicy, perfectly cooked, falling-off-the-bones ribs weren't as tasty as they'd been the last time he was there.

He and Adam discussed the weather, cows and horses and the general life of a rancher, then tentatively planned a fishing trip for late spring. Finally the check came. They split the bill and left, again making the dash to their vehicles a race. This time, Hunter won.

He tipped a finger to his hat and swung out of the parking lot, then turned toward the rolling hills behind the knuckle of lake that jutted north along the highway. He had a couple of things to see to before heading home.

Celia turned off the blow-dryer and listened. Yes, someone was pounding on her door. She laid the dryer aside and ran down the hall to the side door. She flipped on the porch light and peered through the peephole.

Hunter McLean stood on the other side. The snow pelted him with tiny, hard balls, the kind that sting on impact. It built a ridge on his shoulders and the rim of his hat.

"Sissy? I know you're in there!" he yelled.

She looked down at her old pink sweats. There were faded blotches on the front where she'd splashed bleach on them at some point in their long life. She wore thick tube socks. Her hair hung beside her face in wet straight sheets.

"I prefer to be called Celia!" she yelled back.

The silence grew to ominous proportions before he spoke again. "Celia," he said with a great show of patience. "Open up. It's a blizzard out here."

She crossed her arms protectively over her waist. "I'm not dressed for company."

The wind swirled down off the mountains, tossing snow ruthlessly at the man standing on her little stoop. For a minute he disappeared in a cloud of white, but she heard him cursing on the other side of the locked door.

"I need to talk to you!" he shouted over the howl of the wind, the words gritty with his pent-up fury.

"Not tonight," she said stubbornly. "It was a hard day, and I don't feel well."

She wrinkled her nose in distaste. She disliked hiding behind the familiar female lie. But there were times when it was easiest, and this was one of them.

"Dammit, Si— Elia." He caught himself before he used her old school nickname again.

A wry smile curled her lips at his effort not to offend. She stood on her toes and peeked at him again.

The snow was sticking to him now. He looked like Big Foot come to life. She put a hand over her mouth to stifle the laughter. Not that he'd be able to hear it over the whistle of the wind around the corner.

Actually, she had endured a really terrible day. Six kids had come to school with colds and fever. One had been sick in the classroom, which, of course, had upset her none-too-stable stomach and she'd had to make a mad dash down the hall to the bathroom where she'd run into the principal helping an ill third-grader—

"Celia!" It was a roar.

"Oh, all right!" She flung open the door.

Hunter blew in on a swirl of blinding snow. She stepped back as he stamped it off his boots and removed his coat and hat, shedding snow with every movement.

Realizing her toes were getting cold and wet, she retreated into the living room where the fire blazed merrily in the grate. Her hair brushed her cheek in a cold wet lick.

"I'm going to dry my hair," she told Hunter as he emerged like a moth from the white casing of snow.

"Go ahead."

"Grumpus," she muttered to herself.

"What?" He was definitely irritated.

"Grampa Grumpus," she called over her shoulder. "That's what Gran called my grandfather when he was a grouch."

"That's not half what I am at this moment," he warned her in a snarl.

She finished her hair, then put clips in to hold it back at the sides. Her bangs lay in wispy streaks across her forehead. Her face was pale, the freckles standing out across her nose and cheeks like tiny dots drawn on her taut skin. Her fingers trembled when she smoothed lotion on.

When she returned to the living room, she found Hunter had taken his boots off and helped himself to coffee.

"That's leftover from this morning," she said. "I'll make a fresh pot."

"It's okay. I heated it in the microwave."

"Oh." She couldn't think of one thing to say.

He stared at her, his green eyes moody with thoughts that boded no good for her, she was pretty sure. "Sit down," he ordered, noticing her standing there, one foot curled on top of the other one, making an uncomfortable wet place on her sock where she'd stepped into a puddle of melted snow.

"Good idea," she said brightly. Her smile popped up on her face.

He looked taken aback.

"I always smile," she explained, "when I think things are going to be rough."

He frowned.

"It always annoyed my parents, too. It was one thing they agreed on during their marriage." She realized she was rattling on and stopped. She didn't want him to think she was in the least nervous.

The fire crackled loudly while they sat staring at each other. Her smile became determined.

His frown became dangerous.

Chapter Four

Hunter spoke first. "Dawn said you didn't show up Thursday at the nursing home for the exercise classes."

Celia, curled into a corner of the sofa with her feet under her, considered her reply carefully. "That's right."

"She said you dropped the cake off and left before she arrived."

Celia nodded.

"Why didn't you stay?"

She entwined her fingers to hide their shaky state. "I didn't feel like it." She hadn't felt up to dealing with another McLean at that moment, not even one as nice as Dawn usually was.

"Dawn says you aren't a liar."

Celia stared down at her clasped hands. Foreboding crept along her nerves.

"Look at me," he ordered, his voice dropping to a low, almost-sexy rasp.

Meeting the fury in his eyes, she shrank against the sofa cushions. He blinked and the anger was gone.

"Are you pregnant?"

She hesitated, then nodded.

"Is the kid mine?"

She wanted to deny it, but something in his gaze made her pause. She opened her mouth, but no words came. She licked her lips and tried to think of a different tack.

"You don't have to worry," she said at last, her smile in place. "I've decided to sell the house and leave the area. That way, neither of us will be embarrassed by chance meetings."

He ignored her statement. "Is it mine?"

"It's mine," she said defensively, all pretense of civility gone. "The baby is mine."

"And mine."

The fire spluttered and released a jet of flame in a loud hiss. The wind rattled the windowpanes.

"How do you know?" she challenged. "You didn't believe me before. Why should you now?"

He scrubbed his eye sockets with the heels of his hands. "Don't play games. I talked to Adam. He confirmed what you said about leaving with me. Or more aptly, me leaving with you. You drove my truck."

The tiny pellets of snow sounded like BBs as they hit the windows with renewed force. She thought of Hunter driving to the ranch in the dark.

"The storm is getting worse," she told him. "You'd better go home."

"Not until we get this straightened out."

"What?"

He gestured toward her. "You. Me. The baby. I won't have a bastard kid."

Her heart lurched with hope. "Oh. You do believe me about it being yours?"

"I suppose I'll have to. Unless something proves it isn't, I'll have to take your word."

The hope sank into the black ooze of depression. She lifted her chin. "No one will know. I haven't told anyone it was you. Except my mother," she added truthfully.

"Dawn knows," he stated flatly.

"How?" She scrambled through recent conversations, wondering if she'd given her news away inadvertently.

"I told her." His eyes were hooded, shielding his thoughts and his anger. He seemed introspective at the moment. "*She* thinks you're telling the truth."

"I see." She sighed in disappointment.

He flicked her a sardonic glance. He shifted, stretching out his long legs and crossing them at the ankle. Her eyes were drawn to the solid length of him, to the snug V where his legs joined his broad torso.

She recalled the intimacy of feeling every inch of him with every inch of her, of being snuggled against that masculine V, then opening her legs so that the intimacy became even greater....

Glancing up, she saw him watching her. A blush warmed her face. Maybe he'd think it was the firelight reflecting off her skin. She smiled faintly.

He returned it.

Her nervousness increased.

"Okay, then, here's the plan," he said. "We'll drive to Reno tomorrow and get hitched—"

Hitched? She didn't hear what he said after that. "As in 'married'?" she interrupted.

He gave her another sardonic look. "Yes, as in married. Any kid of mine will carry my name."

She shook her head. "No. Oh, no. I couldn't."

"Why not?" He looked mean and dangerous and altogether put out with her.

"Because." She swallowed until her stomach settled back into place. She voiced the first excuse that came to mind. "My mother wouldn't like it."

He muttered an expletive. "What the hell has your mother got to do with it?"

"She told me not to marry you."

Silence pulsed between them. If a granite monolith could swell with rage, he was one. "Who are you going to listen to—her or me?"

"Hmm, well, whoever talks to me last, usually. But I'm agreeing with her."

Her candor seemed to throw him. "You should make up your own mind," he finally said. "Marriage will be better for you."

"I don't see how," she said doubtfully. She considered his offer. Staying on her chosen course seemed much better to her. They were already having a quarrel.

She knew how family fighting affected a child. Parents hadn't a clue how terrible it was for a kid to listen to their arguments day after day—especially those involving who had tricked whom into marriage—and to know he or she was an unwanted complication in their lives and that they hadn't wanted the child or the marriage. She didn't want that for her baby.

He flushed a dark red. "You'll get the McLean name and all that goes with it—money, land, blood-lines that go back to the first settlers."

"Actually, the Campbells were here before the McLeans. Don't you remember the Historical Society presentation on Founders' Day?"

Hunter couldn't believe the earnest gaze she turned on him as she reminded him of the past as if it was imperative that he recall it precisely. She looked so troubled by his sarcastic taunt, he regretted his words.

Her upturned nose with its sprinkle of freckles made her look incredibly young, more like a tomboy than a woman. But only as long as he didn't notice her lush breasts and curvy behind with a nipped-in waist between. She definitely had an hourglass figure.

He cursed again, then stopped when he saw the tremor in her hand as she brushed at her bangs, and the way her gaze flew to the door as if gauging the distance to safety.

She was frightened of him.

The idea amazed him. It irritated him, too. He'd never hurt a woman in his life. Since he hadn't shaken her until her teeth rattled when she'd made her grand announcement at the ranch, why should she be afraid now?

He ran a hand through his hair and tried to see things her way. She'd wanted a kid. She'd chosen him to father it. And had even asked his permission, if she was to be believed. Marriage had evidently not fig-ured into her plans. Okay, so he had been wrong on that score.

"Look," he said, managing a reasonable tone. "It was a hell of a shock for me to meet Jackson and learn my father had another son. It seriously shook my faith in him. Do you think I'd do that to J.J.?"

"I don't think we should marry."

He closed one hand into a fist. He'd never met such a stubborn woman. He couldn't decide if he wanted to shake her or kiss her trembling lips until she quit opposing him.

"I'm trying to be the reasonable one, here." He realized he was almost shouting. He took a breath and tried again. "Why shouldn't we marry? What are your objections?"

He would demolish each one of them. After all, he had logic on his side. Women were emotional creatures at heart. Celia was no different.

"We're already fighting," she told him. "I read that if the seeds are there during courtship..." She frowned slightly. "Well, whatever. Anyway, it would only get worse during marriage. Believe me, I know."

"Why? You been married and no one knows about it?" he asked, deliberately mocking her pretense to know all there was to know about marriage. After all, *he* was the one who'd been married. He knew all about the heaven and hell of it.

"Of course not. I watched my parents' marriage fall apart. It was terrible. I'd never do that to a child."

She was so righteous, he wanted to curse.

She set her rosebud of a mouth and stared at him, as stubborn as an old cow who'd been out on the range too long and didn't figure she had to take orders from any mere human such as him. He'd have to take another tack.

"Excuse me," she said politely, her odd, determined little smile on her face.

He followed when she went into the kitchen and poured a glass of milk and drank it down, one arm pressed across her stomach. He knew about morning sickness and all that.

He waited patiently while she leaned against the counter instead of returning to the sofa. He let his gaze roam over her, assessing her chances of an easy birth the way he would that of a heifer he was thinking of adding to the breeding stock.

Her hips looked wide enough. Her breasts were a nice handful. He paused, startled, wondering if that was a calculated guess or if he knew it from experience.

She observed his every move. Her brown eyes were too big. Her nose was too short, her mouth too cute and her chin too rounded. Her expression was earnest. She didn't look anywhere near thirty and old enough to be a mother. In fact, she reminded him of a teenager down on her luck.

He ambled over to her. She never took her eyes off him. It both amused and annoyed him that he made her nervous. What did she think he would do to her that he apparently hadn't already done?

"You wanted a kid," he said, trying once more to reason with her. "You chose me. Fine. Now it's my turn. We go to Reno tomorrow and do the marriage thing. Understand?"

She nodded slowly, then shook her head.

"Siss—Celia—"

"It would be a mistake. You'd hate being married

to me. I drive people crazy. I dither. And I talk too much when I get nervous.''

"Like now?" he suggested, smiling for the first time with genuine mirth.

"Yes." She rinsed the milk glass and set it aside. No dishwasher, he noted. Now why was that such a surprise?

"Why don't you have a dishwasher?"

"For one person?"

Hmm, she didn't have people sleep over—at least, not often. Maybe she was telling the truth about her love life. Confusion swirled through him, mixing with the black despair that had lived inside him for nearly three years.

"What time do I pick you up tomorrow?"

She looked at him warily and shook her head.

He tamped down the impatience. She was like a wild creature. One wrong move and she'd bolt. Slowly, carefully, never taking his eyes off her, he reached out and brushed a clinging tendril of hair from her cheek.

The warmth of her skin surprised him. He trailed the backs of his fingers along her jaw and down onto her neck. A flush spread into her cheeks. He could barely discern the faint imprint of the freckles.

An image flashed into his mind—of skin that was alabaster white and as smooth as a china cup, small but lush curves that felt perfect under his hand, and heat...the sweet wild heat of passion—

He snapped out of the trance-like state with a jerk of his head. His hand flew back in a reflex action as if he'd burned it when he'd touched her. He stared at her in accusation. Of what, he didn't know.

One thing was for sure—something had happened between them, and he didn't know what it was.

Disoriented, he felt as if he might be drunk, except he hadn't touched a drop in two months. And never would again.

"What time?" he demanded, his voice coming out harsher than he'd intended.

"I think...I'm sure I'm busy tomorrow," she said, edging away from him. She peered at a calendar on the wall next to the phone. "Ah, yes, I am. I have an appointment at the hairdresser's."

She smiled sweetly but regretfully at him. As if the damn hair appointment precluded them going to Reno.

He stalked over to her and stood close, deliberately using his size to intimidate her. He saw her swallow, her big brown eyes going wide.

"We get married tomorrow, or I'll sue for custody of my kid," he threatened, feeling deep within his bones that it was important that his child have his name.

He realized that sometime between her opening the door to him and this very moment, he'd accepted that somehow—and he still wasn't sure how he'd accomplished it—he had conceived a child with this woman.

As strange as that may seem.

She opened her mouth. She immediately snapped her lips together. They turned white from the pressure.

"Hunter, I'm going to be sick," she said, then moaned and pressed the back of her hand to her mouth.

He stepped aside.

She dashed for the bathroom.

"Hell," he said. Talking to her was like trying to spit into the wind. He should just grab her up and haul her off to Reno and be done with it.

Except she seemed to be frightened of him. He'd never had a woman scared of him before. He didn't like it. He'd never hurt anyone that he knew of. Except for a couple of fights with his brother, but that was different.

He sighed and ambled down the hall. He tried the knob and opened the bathroom door. Stepping to her side, he put one hand on her forehead and slid the other across her heaving tummy. He held her until she stopped retching.

After flushing the toilet, he wet a washcloth and wiped her face, then mixed some mouthwash with water and gave her the plastic tumbler. After she'd rinsed, he lifted her into his arms and carried her to bed.

She didn't look at him, but kept her eyes closed the entire time. He set her on the bed, noting that her face was deathly white, her expression one of exhaustion.

"Where's your gown or pj's? he asked.

"Bedside drawer." She barely opened her mouth to speak.

He felt a flicker of pity for her. He personally hated it when he was ill. He retrieved a nightgown from the drawer and began to undress her. He waited for a flash of déjà vu, but nothing came to him.

"I'll do it," she said, taking the gown from him. She disappeared into the bathroom.

In two minutes, she was back. The gown fell to her

ankles. It had long sleeves and a dainty neckline trimmed with lace that hugged her throat. The material was shiny on the outside, but fluffy like flannel on the inside. She looked as woebegone as a lost kitten.

"Very pretty," he said, feeling compelled to say something that would cheer her up.

She didn't look at him. "I think you'd better go, Hunter. I don't think I can talk anymore." She pulled the covers back and climbed into bed without another word. Her face was as pale as her pillowcase.

He studied her while the frustration built. They hadn't gotten a damn thing settled. "I'll see you tomorrow," he said. He waited, but she didn't answer.

Frowning and decidedly irritated, he stomped out after making sure the fire screen was secure and the door locked behind him. As he drove back to the ranch, he tried to envision himself married to Celia Campbell.

The image wouldn't form.

He tried to see her installed at the ranch as his wife. That image wouldn't come, either. It was going to be the worst marriage in history. It was probably a mistake to even consider it. But he couldn't let her go away, taking his kid with her. Marriage. That was the way it would have to be. Lord help them....

Celia glanced out the window. She and Terri and Sheila were having Friday lunch at the restaurant across the road from Honey Lake. They were celebrating the start of spring vacation. She was going to break the news that she had decided to move back to Reno in June.

Now that it was too late, she worried that she was being unfair to bring a child into the world with such an inauspicious beginning. A tremor of unease swept through her.

Across the way, a truck whipped into the parking lot, sending up a splash of mud. Hunter McLean jumped out and slammed the door. She could practically see the anger shimmering around him.

She swallowed as her uneasiness mounted. She'd avoided him for the past week, mostly by screening her phone calls or not answering the door when he knocked.

Yesterday he'd appeared at the nursing home where she worked two days a week doing exercises with the residents. She'd hidden in the linen closet while everyone looked for her. He hadn't found her, thank goodness. The seniors would have relished witnessing a quarrel between her and Hunter. She didn't want to talk to him—

Oh, no, he was heading this way!

She dug out her compact and powdered her nose, then replenished her lipstick, keeping the compact in front of her face so he wouldn't notice her sitting by the window.

When he disappeared, she sighed in relief.

"You can quit hiding," a male voice told her. "I knew you were here. I called first."

She dropped the compact. Hunter picked it up and handed it to her, a mocking smile on his handsome face. "Oh, Hunter, hello," she said, as if surprised to see him.

Her friends echoed the greeting. She saw the curiosity in their eyes as Hunter continued to regard her with that predatory light in his eyes.

"Sorry we can't stay," she said. "We've just finished."

"They are. You're not." He flicked a glance at her friends. "Do you mind? Celia and I have something to discuss."

Sheila looked startled by this announcement. Terri gave Hunter a thoughtful perusal, then stared knowingly at Celia.

Celia met their shocked gazes with a limp smile. "It's nothing," she quickly stated. "I mean, it's a slight misunderstanding."

"We're talking marriage," he said flatly, shocking the waitress as well as the other two women. "I'll take the steak special, lots of fries and a side order of slaw. Beer on tap. We'd like to be alone," he added with a meaningful glance at her friends after rattling off his order.

Celia was appalled. "No, we wouldn't."

"Yes, *darling,* we would." His narrowed eyes dared her to defy him. "I'll take care of the bill," he told the other two.

She realized he wasn't going to be put off. She sat in silent misery while her friends left. The busboy dashed over and cleared a place for Hunter. She pressed a hand to her stomach.

"Queasy?"

"Yes." She glared at him. "I've been fine all week. Until you came around."

His quick grin was unrepentant.

She tried not to notice how gorgeous he looked in his work boots, jeans that fit his lean hips like skin, and a white shirt under a cowhide vest. He'd left his hat in the truck, and his dark hair was ruffled from the wind.

He watched her sip her coffee with a sardonic light in his dark green eyes. "Fox-fire eyes," someone had called them.

She realized, if he'd asked her on New Year's Eve, she would have gladly married him, but now, with his distrust of her, she didn't think a marriage between them stood a chance of working. It was too risky.

"I don't think marriage is a good idea," she said, remembering her mother's lecture two days ago on the hell she'd go through if she married this man.

"Neither do I, but there it is," he said as if it was inevitable and there was nothing else they could do.

"Hunter—"

"You started this. I'm going to finish it. We're going to do the right thing for the kid. No son of mine—"

"It might be a girl."

"Whatever. If it's mine—"

She glared at him.

"All right. I'll take your word for that. We're going to marry, so quit fighting me on it."

The steak-special plate crashed onto the table. The waitress turned red and mumbled an apology. Celia turned green and pressed a hand to her mouth.

Hunter gave the waitress a glance that sent her on her way. He dug into the steak and fries.

"That is just full of cholesterol," Celia told him.

"Yeah, tastes great, doesn't it?"

She sat in stubborn silence while he ate. When the

waitress had taken the empty dishes away and refilled their coffee cups, he leaned back and studied her.

"Marriage," he reiterated softly.

She shook her head.

"You been talking to your mother again?"

"Yes. I spent an evening with her this week."

"I spent most of it sitting in your drive." He scowled. "You're a stubborn critter, Celia."

He sounded surprised. She didn't know whether to be insulted or not.

"I think this would work out," he continued in a musing tone. "My mother left two days ago on a six-month cruise to see the world. I think Jackson deciding to stay at the ranch had something to do with it."

Celia knew it had been a shock to Hunter's mother when her husband had left half the ranch to a bastard son no one had seemed to know about until Mr. Mc-Lean's death. Everyone in the county, herself included, had been dazed by the news.

"With the housekeeper gone, I could use some help," he concluded.

"You want to marry me to get a housekeeper?" She considered throwing the glass of water in his face.

He grimaced impatiently. "It would be easier to hire someone rather than risk marriage."

"So why don't you?"

His pointed gaze swept downward to her tummy, then back to her face. "There are other complications," he continued on a somber note. "J.J. has been diagnosed as possibly autistic. The psychologist thinks we should put him in a special school—"

"Away from his family?" Sympathy for the child

caused her to protest. "No, no, Hunter, don't do that. It would break his heart."

"He's nearly four and he doesn't talk." He shook his head. "He smiles. Sometimes. He can make sounds. I thought I heard him singing in his room a couple of times, but he won't speak."

She recalled the boy and that meeting of the eyes that was like a meeting of their souls.

Hunter sighed. "He watches the world with these big solemn eyes as if he doesn't quite trust it."

"There," she said, resisting an impulse to comfort him. "You see? He hasn't made up his mind to talk yet. I was the same. Except I did talk, but not to my mother for a long time. She didn't want me. Not me personally, but she didn't want children. Oh, Hunter, have you made your son feel you don't want him?"

"No." But a flush of guilt surged into his face.

"Not even when April died?" she prompted. "A child can sense these things, even as a baby."

"I love my son. Why wouldn't I want him?"

"In dealing with your grief, did you withdraw from him?" she asked.

"Maybe. For a while," he admitted. "Dawn and her mom and mine took care of J.J. for most of that year. When the flu went around the next winter, I had to take over. I started taking him with me on the ranch."

"But during that time he would have felt abandoned by the two people who meant the most to him."

Propping her chin on her hand, she thought of the child she carried. She thought of J.J., a lonely little boy who, like her, wasn't sure of his place in the world. She understood his silence.

She told herself it wasn't her problem. She told herself to carry on with her life as she'd planned. She knew she shouldn't be impulsive and softhearted.

Looking up, she saw the darkness in Hunter's eyes as he sat lost in memories. During their night together, he'd spoken of the emptiness within, of loneliness and pain. She'd understood those feelings.

Her heart stirred with pity for him and his son. Life could be so unkind. Perhaps together they could find some degree of happiness. Hope and fear swayed on the balance beam of her emotions.

She wasn't the wife Hunter wanted. She would always come in second to his first marriage. She knew that. Could she accept it?

Yes, if he met her halfway and worked with her. She thought of the coming child, of the little boy whose loneliness had touched her soul, of the man who denied his needs—all of them. Maybe, just maybe, together they could form a family. Others had done it with a lot less going for them. A spark of hope fanned to life inside her.

And because of that faintly glowing spark, she made the decision that would alter their futures forever. "Okay," she said. "I'll marry you."

Chapter Five

"Good. We'll head for Reno as soon as I finish."

Celia gasped. "Not today."

Hunter frowned. "Why not?"

"Well," she said, trying to get her scrambled thoughts in order, "don't you want a prenuptial agreement?"

"No."

His short answer surprised her. "Why not?"

"What good would it do? Anyone who could trick a man into fathering a child without him remembering he did it would know how to get around something as simple as a prenuptial agreement, wouldn't she?"

She swallowed the clog of pain that lodged in her throat. "It wasn't a trick—"

He waved his fork to silence her. "I know. You asked. I agreed. Only why can't I remember anything about it?"

"I don't know," she replied, feeling desolate and filled with worry about the whole situation. Her emotions shifted with the wind, first one way, then another.

"What do you want to do about the wedding?"

For a heartbeat, she thought of white satin and yellow roses, her favorite flower. No use wasting the money. "Let's go to Reno."

"I knew you'd see reason."

"Actually, I'm saving the money for the divorce," she informed him, then regretted the ill humor. Bickering never helped a relationship as far as she could tell.

She sighed at the ridiculous situation. Celia Campbell marrying Hunter McLean. The baby no one had wanted, marrying the prize catch of the county. A sense of foreboding swept over her. She recounted the reasons—his and hers—for the marriage. They sounded logical, and she was trying very hard to be practical. She had to think of the baby's future.

He walked her to her car. "I'll follow you home. We'll go in my truck."

"Okay."

Suspicion darted through his eyes at her acceptance.

She was probably a wuss, but she really didn't mind going along with what others wanted to do. When she tired of people, she left and did her own thing. It was much easier than quarreling. Confrontation made her nervous.

Her mother thought this method of dealing with strife might be a personality defect. Maybe it was, but she didn't know how to be any different.

At her house, she parked in the garage and went inside. She was surveying her clothes when Hunter walked into the bedroom, an irritated expression on his face.

"What are you doing?" he asked.

"Trying to decide what to wear." She held a dress up and studied it.

"What's wrong with what you have on?"

She glanced at her outfit. The slacks were black. The long-sleeved blouse was a rich coppery hue with black trim. "I don't want to be married in this."

"Look—"

"You're not going to change my mind."

He ran a hand through his thick hair, a gesture she thought he used to calm himself. "What happened to the person who went along with whoever talked to her last?"

She pulled out a loosely fitting spring suit she'd bought recently. It was red. "The Chinese marry in red, don't they? Isn't it supposed to bring you luck?"

"How the hell should I know? How long before you'll be ready?"

"Not long. Do you think this is too bold?" She held the red suit up to her and tried to peer into the mirror on the closet door. "You're in the way."

He stepped aside.

She grimaced. "It goes well with my bloodshot eyes."

"Why are your eyes bloodshot?"

"I haven't been sleeping well. I keep dreaming you're going to break into the house and force me to marry you."

He speared her with a dark glance. "No mere man ever forced a female to do anything."

"That's a relief. What do you think?" She held up a pale blue suit from last year. She selected a blouse with a cascade of lace down the front. "White lace and promises. Wasn't that the name of a song?"

"I don't know."

He looked ready to explode, so she grabbed the matching shoes and purse. "I'll only be a minute." She gave him an imploring look.

He hesitated, then stalked out of the bedroom, only to stand in the hallway, his arms folded across his chest in that imperious manner he had.

She slipped out of the slacks and blouse. Holding the suit up, she tried to see herself getting married in it. It didn't seem right. Too somber. She'd gotten it for a charity tea she'd sponsored last spring.

Tiptoeing, she sneaked over to the closet and examined her clothes again. A shimmery material caught her eye. She turned from the suits and day dresses to evening wear. Ah. The Christmas dress from her mom. She'd worn it at New Year's.

It was white gossamer silk, ruffle upon ruffle of it that shifted and shimmered with the slightest movement. It was sleeveless, but the ruffles fell from her shoulders to her elbows. She had a white angora shawl somewhere....

She tiptoed across the room and rooted silently through the chest of drawers.

Hunter peeked around the doorframe. He wouldn't have been surprised to find the window open and his quarry gone.

No, she was there, her back to him, standing in the

bedroom in her skivvies and nothing else. A froth of white stuff was thrown over one arm while she searched through a drawer.

He stared, unable to tear his gaze away. A sheen of sweat broke out all over him.

She had the most delectable figure he'd ever seen in a woman. The curves were lush, and they were in all the right places. Her floral underwear, which looked like a high-cut bikini to him, emphasized the perfection of her body.

While he watched, she pulled a fluffy white shawl from the drawer. Laying it aside, she stepped into the dress and pulled it over her hips. Without any conscious volition on his part, he walked into the room.

When she slid the dress over her arms, he reached into the froth of ruffles and found the zipper.

At his touch, she crossed her arms over her breasts and twisted around to face him. Her eyes were huge, like twin beacons guiding him to...where?

"You're not supposed to be in here," she accused. "You're not supposed to see me."

"Until the ceremony," he murmured. "We still have to drive to Reno. Hold still."

He turned her and zipped the dress, then let his hands drift down her arms and to her waist. The ruffles fluttered under his touch, the material cloud soft. It was like catching a sigh in his hands.

Beneath the cool silk, he felt the warmth of her body. The ruffles shifted over her breasts as she drew a quick breath. He heard his own breaths rasping in his dry throat, the sound loud in the silent room.

She stood perfectly still under his touch, her back to him, her head bent forward as if she contemplated some great platonic question that only the floor could answer. Glancing up, he saw the two of them reflected in the mirror—the small quiet woman, as delicate as a daisy, and his own hulk, broader, darker, more robust than hers.

A tremor coursed through him. His body was strangely quiescent, as if it waited to know what he really wanted before committing itself to passion.

He let her go and stepped back, confused by his own unsettled feelings. ''Are you ready?''

''Almost.''

She cast him a glance, then looked away. He'd never been around a woman as hard to read as this one. He seemed to make her nervous, yet she could hold her ground when she chose; if the outcome was important to her.

It was only when he'd mentioned the coming child and his son that she had agreed to marriage.

Something in him that had been knotted with worry relaxed at this realization. Children obviously meant a lot to her. At least she wasn't a scheming bitch out to get all she could from him, but why had she chosen him to father her child? They'd never been more than casual friends.

He glanced at his watch.

''Hurry,'' he ordered.

Without looking at him, she slipped into white satin pumps, then went into the bathroom. He watched while she smoothed on makeup, then swept her hair into a twist on top of her head. She pulled several strands free so that they fell around her face and neck.

When she finished, he found himself startled by the change. She looked both artless and sophisticated, a study in innocence and allure. Misgivings rose anew in him. She fastened a string of pearls around her neck and pearl studs at her ears, seemingly oblivious to him. Finally she spritzed perfume into the air.

The scent drifted into the bedroom. His body stirred instantly, hungrily, as if the floral essence sparked some primitive memory of passion they had once shared. He rejected it at the same time that he was drawn to her—to the shimmering radiance that spoke of passionate warmth....

"I'm ready," she murmured, not looking at him.

She clutched the white shawl with one hand and headed for the door. He followed. She stopped so suddenly, he nearly plowed into her.

"What?" he asked in a much harsher tone than he'd intended.

Her hand fluttered nervously, indicating the bedroom. "My clothes. I have to have clothes."

"We'll get them tomorrow."

"I'll need an overnight case." She rushed to the closet and retrieved a small bag.

"We can spend the night here, I suppose." He'd have to call Dawn and ask her to keep J.J., which was no problem. The kid loved staying with her.

Celia stared at him as if he'd suggested something decadent. "The bed's too short."

It was obvious she didn't want him here. He bit back a smart retort about having shared a smaller bed than that with a woman and not getting any complaints out of her.

He didn't figure his bride-to-be wanted to hear about his past experience. Give him credit for some finesse. Besides, she looked as if she might bolt at any moment. He didn't intend to give her cause.

Now that he'd decided to marry her, he wanted to get the deed done and behind him.

"I'll pack some things." She opened the case and quickly loaded it with toiletries, a nightgown, a change of clothing and sneakers.

"We can stay in Reno," he said, making the decision. "I'll call Dawn and ask her to keep J.J. for the night."

Celia looked doubtful, which firmed his resolve that this was the best solution. He didn't relish a quick marriage, then an immediate return to the ranch and the questions he would face. The internal blackness shifted precariously at the thought of arriving home with a strange woman in tow.

He looked at her flat tummy. No kid of his was going to be born a bastard. If she said the kid was his—and Dawn thought it must be—he'd accept it. If he found out differently, he'd divorce her in a New York minute.

"Let's go." He took the case and ushered her out before she thought of something else to do.

She was silent on the ride to Highway 395. He was grateful for small favors. He called his sister-in-law and made arrangements for his son. That finished, he tried to think of something to say.

Celia watched the scenery speeding by without one glance in his direction. She looked neither happy nor upset. "Resigned" might be a better description.

"Why, Celia?" he finally asked.

She didn't pretend to misunderstand the question. "I wanted a child. You were available. I figured no one would get hurt since both of us were unattached. I mean, with Dawn marrying your half brother..."

Her voice trailed off as if she were afraid she would hurt his feelings. Everyone had expected him to marry Dawn.

"She's happy. I'm happy for her," he said.

Celia gave him a relieved smile. "Aren't they handsome together, her so fair and him so dark and fierce and protective? Their wedding was beautiful. I wish—"

He cast her an inquiring glance. She was staring into space, a raw yearning in her eyes. It made him uneasy, as if she hurt inside the way he sometimes did. "You wish?"

"Nothing. No one will believe I've caught the most eligible bachelor in the county, will they?" Her smile popped up, chipper than a robin in a spring meadow. He must have imagined the other.

"Who gives a damn what anyone believes? If they ask why we married, tell them it's none of their business."

The smile faded. The brightness dimmed. Even the shimmery dress seemed to darken. He felt like Scrooge.

"I doubt anyone will care," she said quietly. She was silent again as they sped toward Reno. "Do you mind if I call my mother?" she asked as they neared the city.

"Will you let her talk you out of this?"

"No. I always keep my word once I give it. It's a character flaw of mine."

He handed over the cell phone. She made the call, broke her news, then invited her mother to join them.

"Where?" she asked, pressing the phone to her shoulder.

He recalled the name of a chapel down the street from the hotel. "Bower of the Heart."

Her eyes widened. "How apropos," she murmured. She repeated it to her mother, ironic humor tripping through her voice. He was glad she found it so amusing.

Since her mother had requested thirty minutes to get ready, he went straight to the hotel and checked them in.

"Mr. and Mrs. McLean," the desk clerk repeated. The man looked at him with a bland expression. "Will you need a bellman for your luggage?" He craned his neck to peer at the one small case Hunter carried.

He felt they were there under fraudulent pretenses. He set his jaw, took the card keys, handed one to Celia and led the way to the elevator.

Their room was on the fourteenth floor. The king-size bed looked shockingly huge when he entered. Celia went to the bathroom and closed the door. He set the case down and went to the window.

Gazing at the hills surrounding the town, he wondered what he was letting himself in for with this rash marriage. The first time had been so different—all sweet anticipation and fierce pride that he and April would be bound legally, husband and wife before all the world. Now he felt only resignation. He glanced at his watch.

"Celia," he called.

The door opened slowly, reinforcing the fact that she wanted this even less than he did. Too bad. She'd gotten herself into this neat little mess. She'd have to bite the bullet just as he was doing.

"Ready?"

She nodded and preceded him out when he held the door. They walked the block down to the chapel. Her mother was there, a quick, nervous woman who puffed angrily on a long, thin cigarette. She ground it out when she saw them.

"Are you going through with this?" she demanded of her daughter after giving him a dirty look.

She made him feel like crawling back under the rock he came from until he reminded himself that he hadn't asked for this. "It's time," he interrupted.

Celia had her lips clenched and again looked as if she might bolt at any moment. He took each woman by the arm and ushered them inside. A grandfatherly man in a dark suit came forward.

"Welcome to the Bower of the Heart," he said in a deep, reassuring voice that was rather hushed and soothing.

He reminded Hunter of a funeral-parlor director.

"Are we here for a ceremony?" the man inquired, his gaze moving from Celia's fluttery white dress to Hunter's work clothes and scuffed boots.

Hunter felt his ears warm. Hell, he probably should have taken the time to stop by the ranch and change clothes. It hadn't occurred to him to dress up for what he'd assumed would be a tussle with Celia over the marriage.

"Yes," he said before Celia's mother said something.

"Ah, would the bride care for flowers? We have some lovely bouquets." The man gave them a coy smile and deftly maneuvered Celia over to a display cooler.

She selected a bunch of yellow roses mixed with tiny white flowers. The man pinned a pink-and-white corsage to Mrs. Campbell's pink wool suit, then studied him, a yellow boutonniere in hand, as if wondering where to put it.

Hunter grabbed the damn thing and stuck it through the buttonhole on the leather vest he wore. "Are we ready now?" he asked, unable to keep the sarcasm from coming through.

Celia's mother gave him another of her drop-dead glances, then fussed with her daughter's dress, arranging the ruffles and fluffing the back of the skirt.

"We're ready," Celia announced in a surprisingly firm voice. She took his arm and faced the justice of the peace.

Her mother stood beside her. The JP called a woman from the back, who took her place behind him. The ceremony took little more than a minute. Hunter realized he hadn't thought of rings. He slipped his college-graduation ring off and put it on Celia's finger when the man asked for it.

She closed her hand to keep it from sliding off. As soon as the JP finished, she handed it back. Her fingers were icy cold when she touched him.

"Just a minute and I'll have the papers," the man announced. When he was through, they signed the document that made them husband and wife in the eyes of the law. Mrs. Campbell and the other woman signed as witnesses and the JP as the ministering officer.

They left amid farewells and wishes for their happiness. Standing on the sidewalk, the three looked at each other. He wondered what came next.

"Well, I suppose we can go to the hotel," he said.

Mrs. Campbell looked at him as if he'd suggested he would perform indecent acts on her daughter right there in the street.

"Yes," Celia agreed unexpectedly. "I'd like to lie down. Thank you for coming, Mother." She kissed her mother's cheek, then took his arm and they headed back toward the hotel. She looked pale to him.

"Are you going to be sick?" he asked.

"I don't know." She stared grimly ahead.

At the hotel, the doorman smiled expansively when he spotted them. "Congratulations," he said.

"Thank you," Celia replied graciously.

The bellman also congratulated them. Several strangers did the same.

"It's the flowers," he decided. He threw the boutonniere into a trash can and reached for the roses she clutched to her chest.

"Don't."

The one word, uttered with dead seriousness, stopped him. She didn't glance his way. "All right, then." He wasn't sure, but he thought he'd just lost the first battle of their marriage.

In the room, he sat down by the window. She put her bouquet in a glass of water.

After removing the shimmery white dress, she slipped under the covers and closed her eyes with a weary sigh.

After a while, he realized she was asleep. He quietly left the room and went to the casino. There he played machine poker for several hours, losing track of time until he realized it had grown dark outside.

Glancing at his watch, he saw it was after six. He'd better see about dinner for his bride. He found her still asleep when he entered the dark room. He bent over her, worried that she might be sick.

She opened her eyes. "Oh," she said, startled.

"Sorry. I was wondering if I should wake you. It's time to eat. I could have something sent up."

"Pizza," she promptly said. "I'd kill for a pizza. I'll take a diet soda, too."

"Okay, pizza it is." He put in the order.

She sat up. The sheet pooled at her waist. The pastel design of her bra reminded him of the wildflowers that grew on the ranch, her skin a pale background for the lush profusion of blossoms.

For a second, the strangest thing happened. He could imagine— No, it was stronger than that. He could feel the way her breasts beaded under his touch, could taste the sweet nectar of her pink nipples in his mouth....

Hot, turgid blood beat through him, making him dizzy as needs he hadn't felt in years flooded him.

She pulled the sheet up to her shoulders, and the sensation blinked out of his mind like a dream that had never been.

Or had it?

Confusion swirled through his mind. The images had seemed more than imagination, but he couldn't credit them with reality. He felt odd, off-balance—

"What have you been doing?" she asked. Her knees poked against the sheet as she drew her legs up. She propped her elbows on them. She looked tired, young and vulnerable.

"Playing the slots. I won five dollars." He turned back to the window, but that didn't shut out the knowledge that he was alone in a bedroom with a woman.

His wife.

The words singed his insides. They seemed alien to him, as alien as being with a woman in a hotel room. He inhaled deeply and tried to release the tension when he exhaled.

A knock at the door distracted him. Celia leaped from the bed and rushed into the bathroom. He answered the door and paid for the room service.

"All clear," he called.

She returned, dressed in a thick white robe. She rubbed her eyes and patted back a yawn. She settled in a chair beside the cart. "You ready to eat?"

"Yeah." He took the other chair.

She served him, then herself. He noticed the way the robe gaped open at the neckline. It was much too large for her small proportions. She looked like a girl playing dress-up in an adult's clothing.

Yet there was nothing girlish about her curves.

He took a bite of pizza, noticing that her inner thigh was visible almost to the apex of her legs when she curled her feet under her and stared out at the night while she ate. His mouth went dry as heat spiraled through him.

Strange to have these sensations now. No woman had turned him on in nearly three years. Sis—*Celia* wasn't the type to attract him, yet he found himself in a state of...not exactly arousal, but there was definitely interest. It just didn't add up.

Restless, he finished off half the pizza, drained his cola, then returned to the window, aware of her silent scrutiny. He turned to face her.

She gazed up at him, the golden flecks in her light brown eyes picking up the glow from the hanging lamp. Her lips were a soft, natural pink. She looked drowsy and content the way a woman sometimes did after an especially satisfying bout of lovemaking.

The heat exploded into a volcano. He sucked in air. It did no good. He headed for the door. "I think I'll take a walk." He left the room.

Celia stared at the door for a long time after Hunter left. She ate another piece of pizza, finished the soft drink, then pushed the cart into the hall. She didn't want to wake to the smell of cold pizza in the morning. Just thinking of it made her ill.

She grimaced at the vagaries of being pregnant. After watching the news and a special on public television, then a nature show on a cable channel, she changed into her nightgown, washed up and went to bed.

Since being pregnant, she noticed she tended to sleep a lot more. She wondered if it would be gauche to fall asleep on her wedding night before the groom returned. She leafed through a magazine.

He'd given her some odd glances since they'd arrived back at the hotel as husband and wife. She tried to decide whether he wanted her and wasn't sure she would welcome him, or if he didn't and wasn't sure how to make his feelings clear.

She thought over her own feelings. Memories

crowded in. He'd been so gentle when he'd lain down beside her on her bed at New Year's. He'd smoothed her hair back.

"You have such fine hair," he'd remarked, letting a curl twine around his finger.

"It tends to fly away." She'd been breathless, still not quite believing she was with Hunter and what was about to happen between them. This, even though both of them were naked. It was intensely exciting.

"Is it naturally curly?"

"Yes, but I get a soft perm a couple of times a year to make it more manageable," she'd said in her usual truthful-to-the-point-of-absurdity manner. He hadn't been interested in the details of her hair care.

However, he'd nodded as if he understood.

After tracing the line of her eyebrows, down her nose and over her lips, he'd finally run his finger along her chin and throat. "What have we here?" he'd asked, a smile curving his lips, his eyes slumberous.

"What?" she'd asked.

"Two lumps." His expression had teased as he'd explored her chest. "We'd better see what these are. It could be serious." Then he'd tugged the sheet down until he could gaze at her torso.

The lazy gleam of sexy humor had disappeared, to be replaced by the flames of passion as he'd bent his head and kissed her, first on one breast, then the other.

Heat coiled deep within her as she recalled all the things he'd done to her that night—not once, but twice. She understood why the French called it "the little death."

For those moments in his arms, she'd lost all

awareness of the world, or even of herself and him as separate persons. The point where they merged had become the point of existence as spangles of white-hot light filled the darkness behind her closed eyelids and she'd cried out his name in the sweet delirium of release.

Ah, but she'd loved him in those passion-crazed moments. When she'd finally dropped into an exhausted sleep, he'd left her, slipping out into the night without a goodbye. Sometimes she thought she'd dreamed it.

She laid a hand over her abdomen. No, not dreamed. This was reality. She sighed and frowned at the door, wondering where he was. Would he go to another woman?

The thought hurt, but only for a moment. Hunter wouldn't disregard their vows. She was as sure of that as she was of the sunrise.

Finally, she turned out the lamp, leaving a night-light on for her errant husband. Well, so much for the wedding night. There would be other nights between them.

She reminded herself that a clean slate started with each morning. Tomorrow would be different from any she'd ever faced. Her heart jumped between fear and elation in noisy confusion.

Married to Hunter. Who would believe it?

She considered the possibilities and the future they would make together. Her qualms gradually smoothed out, and she went to sleep.

Chapter Six

The pickup bounced across a rut in the graveled area between the ranch buildings and the house. Celia held on to the seat as she swayed from side to side. She'd eaten toast for breakfast, but still she felt queasy.

"I'll have Tom grade the ranch roads as soon as the weather clears," Hunter said. He spoke as if she'd complained about the ruts.

"Good idea," she said, determined to be cheerful.

He had hardly glanced at her that morning. His eyes were bloodshot and red-rimmed. She thought he'd stayed in the casino all night, but since she'd slept until seven that morning, she wasn't sure. He'd been in the room, drinking coffee and reading the paper when she awoke.

She rubbed the chills from her arms as she recalled waking and finding him there, looking as if he'd battled death and barely won. To her surprise, he'd been kind.

He'd given her a piece of dry toast and told her to stay in bed and chew on that until her stomach settled down.

It had worked. She'd followed his instructions and hadn't been sick as soon as her feet touched the floor for the first time in weeks. There were advantages to marrying an experienced man.

And heartache, too.

She wondered if he'd spent the night remembering his first wedding night. He'd been so full of despair on New Year's Eve, so lonely.

Her hand lifted, ready to touch him and offer comfort. She caught herself in time. Since their wedding, he'd closed himself off from her entirely, his thoughts shielded behind a curtain of control that told her not to meddle. She would respect that, but they needed to talk about their future.

"Tomorrow is another day, as Scarlett O'Hara would say," she murmured. "It's up to us what we make of it. Don't you agree?"

That stirred him out of his introspection. "What?"

"The future. It's up to us what we make of it. We can work together...or we can make each other miserable."

He parked the truck near the patio that wrapped around two sides of the modern ranch house, turned off the ignition and perused her with a skeptical expression.

"You think we should make the best of a bad situation?" he asked. "I suppose we have to."

"Ouch," she said. She pulled an imaginary dart

from her chest. "Should I wear a flak jacket when we're together?"

Silence beat between them, heavy as the air before a storm. "Sorry," he said at last.

Darkness crowded into his eyes, reminding her there was no joy in her husband at this rushed marriage. She wasn't feeling very sure about it herself at the moment.

An elopement. Her friends would be blown right out of their minds when she told them.

She determined to look on the bright side. "That's okay. If we remember to be kind, things should work out. I read that once. A marriage counselor advised this couple to be as kind to each other as they would be to their friends. He said people shouldn't say cruel things and not expect others to retaliate." She shut up when she caught him watching her as if he couldn't believe how naive she was.

"Is that the end of today's lesson in Marriage 101?"

She refused to be daunted by the sarcastic barb. "Yes." She smiled at him.

He blinked, then shook his head slightly.

"That's okay. My parents sometimes thought I was a tad odd, too. You'll get used to it."

"To what?"

"Me. I smile when I get nervous. And talk too much. It's because I want everyone to be friends. I wanted it for my parents most of all."

For a second, she remembered the times she'd gone to her room and cried while her parents fought. She wanted a different life for her child.

Looking at her handsome husband, she wistfully

thought of the life they could have together—if they loved each other....

He eyed her once more, then swung out of the truck. He grabbed her lone piece of luggage and slammed the door. When he bounded onto the patio and headed for the house, she realized he assumed she would follow.

So much for her sermon on niceties. She climbed down and crossed the patio. He stood at the door.

"Do you want me to carry you across the threshold?" he asked unexpectedly, but with a sharp edge as if he mocked her efforts at civility.

She considered. "Maybe that would be a good idea." It might help get them off on a better footing.

He placed the overnight case inside on the floor, then swung her up into his arms. "You weigh less than a bale of straw," he said, a scowl cutting a line between his eyes.

"I've lost five pounds."

His gaze met hers as he stepped into the warm kitchen. He kicked the door closed behind them, then stood there as if she was an impulse buy and he wasn't quite sure where to store her now that he had her home. He set her down abruptly and picked up the case.

"This way."

She kept close as they went up the steps to the second floor. He showed her into a pretty bedroom that she knew instinctively was for guests. "Where do you sleep?"

"Across the hall. J.J.'s room is at the end." He tilted his head in that direction and placed her case on a parson's bench against the wall. "I have work to do."

He left her. She had a glimpse of a king-size bed with a blue comforter, blue drapes closed against the morning sun and a rocker/recliner next to a square oak table before he closed the door to the master suite.

The emptiness of the guest room enfolded her. How odd, she mused, to be the outsider in her own marriage just as she'd been in her parents'.

"You'll never feel unwanted," she promised the baby growing inside her. "No one will hurt you."

For a moment, all the dreams she'd ever had rose in her, pressing on her heart until she ached with the terrible pain of never-satisfied yearning. She sighed shakily, no longer sure she and Hunter could make it—not even by being kind to each other.

She gazed around the room. Heavy satin curtains in beige and gold covered the windows. She opened them and found gold sheers underneath.

Peering outside, she noted the room was on the west side of the house. She liked the east so that she woke with the morning sun. She couldn't see any activity from here.

Instead of facing the barns and stables where the ranch chores were centered, her room looked out on the orchards. The apple and pear trees had buds. The cherry tree was ready to burst into bloom.

Hearing Hunter's door open, she rushed into the hall in time to see him disappear down the stairs. She followed and caught up with him in the kitchen. He leaned against the wall and tugged on his boots.

"Is this to be our marriage?" she asked. "Separate rooms? Are we to be polite strangers? Do we speak when we meet on the stairs?'' According to all she'd read, this was not a good start to building a relationship.

He straightened and eyed her grimly. ''I don't know,'' he admitted. ''Look, I know this is... strange.''

''It is,'' she agreed. ''We should make our marriage as normal as possible for it to succeed.''

''It can't be normal.'' He gave her a glance of pure frustration. ''Don't you understand?''

She shook her head.

''I don't know how anything happened between us that night. I haven't been able to—'' He broke off, his eyes dark with anger and a bleakness she couldn't fathom. ''I told you. I haven't been with a woman in over two years.''

''Until New Year's Eve,'' she corrected, refusing to let him deny their time together.

''Evidently,'' he agreed. ''I've accepted what must have happened. But now there's nothing. I don't feel a thing.''

Hunter paused. He had felt something—not full-fledged desire, but he had experienced a stirring of the blood at the sight of Celia's delicate body and shimmering radiance as she'd prepared for their impromptu wedding.

''Oh.'' A blush tinged her cheeks in a ruddy sweep. Her stubborn smile wavered, then righted itself.

He admired her fortitude. She apparently had no idea of the strange bargain she'd made when she'd married him. In fact, she looked too innocent to even comprehend the extent of their problems.

There was nothing of the artless sophisticate about

her today. Dressed in jeans and sneakers, with an oversize peach shirt, her hair clipped back with white barrettes, she could have passed for sixteen. Maybe.

The blackness ate a hole in his soul. He didn't want to feel anything for her—not pity, not admiration, certainly not desire. He'd been through that hell. Never again.

"I've got work to do," he muttered, angry with her, with himself and most of all with the fate that had taken the good things from him and shrouded his soul in a darkness and despair that nothing could penetrate.

"What time will you be in for lunch?" she asked.

"I'll skip it."

She blinked as if he'd slapped her. He turned away from her and the smile that wouldn't die, refusing to acknowledge the vulnerability that had flashed through her eyes.

"I need my clothes from the other house," she said, recovering in an instant. "And my car."

He shrugged into a heavy coat and jammed his hat on. "We'll go to town in the morning. There'll be four hands besides me for dinner. And J.J. I'll pick him up before I come in around six." He gave her a frowning perusal. "Do you think you could fix sandwiches?"

"Yes."

"Good." He walked out.

Celia sat down on the chair she'd perched on the day she'd come to tell him her news. The silence of the kitchen crowded around her. She could hear her heartbeat—an unsteady *thunk* in her chest. She pressed a hand there, suddenly frightened of the future the way she'd been when her father had left them.

She believed what she'd said about making the best of things, about being kind and all that, but she had realized something in the past few minutes.

Hunter had a winter heart. It was encased in arctic ice and the darkness of eternal midnight. Their moments together on New Year's Eve had been a false spring. The thaw had lasted only the one night.

Her stricken gaze drifted over the attractive green-and-white decor. She went to stand in the sunshine that streamed through the windows onto the counter like a benediction.

She exhaled shakily and recalled that she had five men to feed. She wasn't born to it, but she would try to be a good rancher's wife. She could cook. That might surprise him.

She lifted her face to the sun and sought the hope that sustained her when life got too rough. "Today," she said to the silent house, "is the first day of the rest of our lives." She would try to make it a good one.

Celia almost missed the knock on the door as she whirled the vacuum cleaner over the carpet. She turned off the machine and listened. A second knock sent her hurrying to the kitchen door.

Through the glass she saw Dawn McLean. They were neighbors now. Celia envisioned morning coffee and friendly chats. The possibilities for friendship pleased her.

When she opened the door, Hunter's son stood beside his aunt. A black dog sat beside the boy. "Dawn.

J.J. Come in. You're my very first visitor." She swept into a curtsy, then swayed a little as dizziness washed over her.

"Are you okay?" Dawn took her arm.

"I forgot to eat lunch. I've been so busy." She waved a hand to indicate the work she'd accomplished. "Everything was dusty." She closed the door behind them.

"It's been a while since Hunter had a housekeeper. Are you sure you should be doing all this work?" Dawn hung up their coats.

Celia recalled that Dawn knew of her condition. A blush worked its way into her cheeks. She smiled brightly. "I'm fine. Did you see Hunter?"

"Yes. He told me you and he were married in Reno yesterday." Dawn's grin was wry. "Did Hunter give you time to invite anyone to the ceremony?"

"My mother came. I had yellow roses with white baby's breath. It was very nice." Celia realized she was fluttering nervously. She knelt in front of J.J., who had stared at her from the moment he walked in with his young-old eyes. "Would you like a cookie? I found some in the pantry earlier."

He nodded.

She gave him her very brightest smile. She poured milk for her and J.J., coffee for Dawn, then set a plate of cookies out. "Help yourself. I'm going to have a sandwich. Would you like one?"

"We've had lunch," Dawn told her. "The house looks different. Brighter."

"I opened all the drapes."

It was odd, but pleasant, to sit in the kitchen that

was now hers, and chat with Dawn. J.J. ate two cookies and drank all his milk. That made her feel good.

"It's time for his nap," Dawn explained. "I told Hunter I'd put him down, then I need to go to town. Do you want anything?"

"No, thanks. Hunter and I are going tomorrow to pick up my clothes. I'll get my car and stop by the store."

She replaced the vacuum in the closet while Dawn tucked J.J. into his bed. After the other woman left, Celia dusted the furniture, then checked the crown roast in the oven. The potatoes and carrots were browning nicely. The green beans were ready to be turned on.

After icing the chocolate-pudding cake, she tiptoed down the hall. J.J. was sleeping like an angel. She took a quick shower and slipped back into her jeans and shirt. She patted on makeup and put her hair up, which made her look more mature, she thought. She spritzed cologne around her.

There, she was ready for her first dinner as a married woman. Chill bumps popped out all over her arms and neck.

Hunter closed the stable door and glanced at the house. His heart gave a gigantic lurch. He stopped abruptly as a mixture of unidentified emotions sliced through him.

Light spilled from the windows, beacons to brightness and the warmth inside. It was the way the place had looked when April had been there, ready to welcome him home, into her arms and the special haven of their love and happiness.

He closed his eyes against the pain that would roll over him in the next few seconds—expecting it, wanting it. At one time it was all that had told him he was alive.

The agony didn't hit with the straight-on-a-nerve impact it once had. There had been that first lurch, then those other feelings, all in a jumble he couldn't sort through.

He walked slowly up the driveway. When he stepped foot on the planking, he paused. Inside he could see the woman he'd married moving around. Then she disappeared.

His body stirred unexpectedly, making him feel as if an alien occupied his skin. The pang of excitement was not exactly unwelcome. After all, he was a healthy male. Rather, it surprised him. His new wife wasn't what he wanted. That was why the hunger came as such a shock.

Another of those strange images came to him. He saw a woman in a white dress, the kind Celia had worn for the wedding. She was in his arms. He had an impression of music. He tried to see her face, but couldn't.

Longing hit him, along with the raw need he couldn't seem to control. He wanted to touch that image and feel the shimmering warmth of her body through the silk. He wanted to bury himself in that warmth until the cold left him....

He shoved the thought aside and sought the safety of the blackness where no emotion dwelled. He didn't need this—not now, not ever.

Striding across the patio, he threw open the door

and entered the house. The smells and sounds that hit his nose and ears jarred him.

The aroma of food. The soft sounds of music.

For the first time in years, the house felt welcoming to him. It felt like home. Something warm and bright tugged at his insides. Not pain this time.

He paused, waiting, unsure what it was. Then it was gone. Frowning, he tugged off his boots, hung up his outside clothing and went into the dining room to see what the hell was going on.

"Hi," Celia said. She glanced up from the candles she was lighting. Her smile was soft, sexy.

The table was set with his mother's best china and a lace tablecloth. A bottle of California Merlot was open and ready to pour. J.J. was folding napkins and placing them under the forks with studious attention.

"Dawn dropped J.J. by for his nap," Celia informed him. "He's been helping me."

Hunter realized he should have given Celia some notice about what to expect. Fury at his own stupidity and at her romantic preparations made his tone harsher than he meant it to be. "You think cowboys are going to spend a hard day moving cattle, then dress up for dinner when they come in at night?" He gestured toward the table. "Whatever possessed you to go to these extremes?"

She and J.J. went big-eyed, like two kids caught in some act that had been forbidden them. His son moved closer to Celia, his gaze on the floor.

"It was our first dinner—I mean, as bride and groom…in our home…."

"Cowboys like simple fare, and plenty of it. Do you have enough food?" He tried not to notice the way the shine left her eyes as she shook the match out.

The smile returned, but it was subdued. "Yes. Will they be here soon?"

"Yeah. They'll wash up before they come over."

He spun around and headed for his bedroom. There was something disturbing in the way she held her head high and went right on with her ridiculous preparations.

Candles. Cloth napkins. The formal dining room.

The ranch hands would be shocked out of their minds. It would be a miserable meal. Hell, she should have known better than to go with the fancy stuff for a bunch of cowboys. April would have— No, that wasn't fair.

April had been born on the ranch down the road. Celia had lived her life in town. Two different worlds. A sigh worked its way up from his toes.

After a quick shower, he debated with himself on what to wear. Finally, as a concession to her efforts, he put on dress slacks and a white shirt. Rolling the sleeves up, he returned to the dining room. He supposed he'd have to help her pull this off.

Laughter came from the kitchen. Hunter followed the sound. Tom, an old cowboy who had stayed on to help out over the winter, lifted a roast from the pan onto a meat platter. Celia, a wet paper towel held to her finger, was laughing and directing the men.

Hunter leaned against the doorway and watched in open amazement as his cowhands made fools of themselves.

"Rick," his wife ordered, "open these crab-apple

slices and put them around the roast when Tom gets it on the plate. That will make a nice color contrast.''

''I sure hope he doesn't drop it,'' Rick said, giving old Tom a worried glance. ''That's the best-looking piece of meat I've seen in an age.''

Pete, their newest hand and the youngest cowboy there, hooted. ''You were eyeing that little gal at Scudder's Inn like you thought she was the best-looking piece of—''

A loud harrumphing from Tom cut off the rest of that statement. ''You boys stand back,'' he ordered. ''I'm taking this platter to the table. We can carve the roast there.''

''Oh, good idea!'' Celia exclaimed as if the old cowboy had just discovered the moon. ''Rick, those two bowls of vegetables are ready. J.J., can you carry the rolls? Be careful, they're hot.''

''Here, let me carry something.'' Pete had a tussle with Rick over the green beans but finally won out.

Jason, the bashful cowboy and the quietest, removed plates of salad from the refrigerator.

Hunter watched in amazement as four grown men fell all over each other trying to get dinner on the table.

''What happened to your hand?'' he asked.

Silence fell like a prayer shawl over the room.

Celia held her index finger out for his inspection. ''I burned it on the roast pan.''

''She nearly dropped the danged thing,'' Tom chimed in. ''It's too heavy for a little gal like her.''

Hunter snorted when Celia smiled prettily at the old buzzard, which caused him to nearly trip over his own feet and drop the roast, platter and all.

She steadied the old man with a hand on his arm. "Everyone has been so helpful."

"Except me," Hunter mumbled, irritated by the whole lot of them, including his son, who carried the wooden bowl of rolls as if it contained the crown jewels.

In another moment, she had everyone at the table and seated. Somehow she managed to direct them and look helpless and fluttery at the same time.

"Your place is at the end," she said.

A lock of blond-streaked hair wafted over her left eye, enticing him to tuck it back in the bunch on top of her head. He reached out, then jerked his hand back.

She looked as innocent as a newborn, but he'd seen her arrange her hair in that artless manner for their wedding. It was as calculated as a battle plan.

And maybe she'd planned their marriage with the same deliberation. Maybe she'd known he would never spring a surprise brother on *his* son.

Her stubborn smile stayed in place when he scowled at her. He took his seat without comment.

Tom nudged him under the table. "You're supposed to carve the roast the little lady fixed for us."

"Laying it on pretty thick, old man," he told his oldest ranch hand.

Tom grinned. "Maybe you don't know how to do something that takes a little finesse and all. Maybe I should show you youngsters how it's done."

Hunter grabbed up the meat fork and carving knife. He tested the blade. Razor sharp. He sliced into the roast and slapped the meat on a plate.

"Pass this to my wife," he told Tom, "and try not to drool over it—or her, if you can help it."

"I'm not the one acting like a bull with one cow," Tom said with self-righteous dignity.

The three cowboys guffawed. Celia laughed as loud as the men. Even J.J. grinned. Hunter felt his ears burn. He snorted and cut into the succulent meat. Dinner took an hour to consume. The dessert was the best they'd ever eaten, all four men declared. They helped carry the dishes to the sink.

After they trooped out, Celia cleaned the kitchen.

Hunter rammed his fingers into his back pockets and watched her. She cast him a self-conscious glance a couple of times, but went on with her work.

J.J. put the silverware into the basket.

"What?" she finally asked.

"You pulled that one out of the fire," he commented, disgruntled with the whole evening, feeling put out and left out, although he'd been there the entire time.

"Meaning?"

"You had the men eating out of your hand in five minutes flat. That was an impressive show. Burning your finger was an inspiration. Was it real? Or was it planned?"

She stuck the last plate in place, thanked J.J. for his help and closed the dishwasher. When she looked at him, her expression was blank. "What do you think?"

"I don't know," he admitted.

"Are you going to get J.J. ready for bed or shall I?" she asked, her tone going softer as she looked at the boy.

Hunter scooped his son up. "I'll do it."

"Good. I'll finish in here."

When he returned to the living room, which his mother called the "great room" because of its vaulted ceiling and large size, Celia was on the sofa, her feet tucked under her satiny nightgown. She was reading a ranching magazine.

She glanced up at his entry. "It was mostly pretense," she said. "The burned finger and helpless act. I read that giving people something to do makes them feel more at ease, as if they're part of the group. It seemed to work."

"Was your pregnancy as calculated as the burned finger?" he asked, anger at a slow boil inside him. He'd given up trying to figure out why and simply acted on it.

She met his gaze levelly. "I never asked for marriage."

"But knowing my past, didn't you also know, or suspect, that I would insist on it?"

"Oh, yes," she said in that bright tone she adopted when cornered. "I planned it all."

She folded her hands in her lap and sat there as serene as a Christmas-tree angel.

He was shocked by the admission. And baffled. Why the hell didn't she defend herself or at least yell at him? He realized she wasn't going to argue. That made him more frustrated.

Spinning, he slammed out of the house, forgetting the night and the cold until it chilled him straight to the bone. He cleaned and oiled tack in the stable until the light went out in the living room.

* * *

Celia opened her eyes when she felt someone sit on the end of the bed. J.J., dressed in blue cords and a red, blue and yellow top, perched on the mattress. He crossed one leg over the other, propped his chin on his hand and stared at her with hardly a blink.

She closed her eyes, knowing if she so much as lifted her head, she'd be sick. "Hi," she said. "I can't get up. I forgot the crackers last night when I came to bed."

That was because she was mad at his father, but she didn't say so. The child had enough worries.

The bed shifted. Her stomach tilted. She gritted her teeth and hung on. Running feet receded from her hearing. A minute later, something touched her shoulder.

Opening her eyes, she spied a cracker two inches from her nose. She accepted it and munched in tiny bites until it was gone. Ten minutes later, she felt fine. Throwing back the covers, she gingerly sat up.

"That worked," she told the boy and gave him her biggest smile. "My tummy liked that cracker. You were very nice to bring it to me."

He peered at her for a long minute, then he smiled in his solemn manner.

"Well, I suppose it's time to get up and greet the day." She checked the clock. "Seven. What does one do at this hour on a ranch?"

He pointed downstairs.

"Breakfast, right? Have you eaten?"

He shook his head. Hunter was probably up and out doing whatever ranchers did. She went into the bathroom.

J.J. was waiting when she was ready to face the

world in general and his daddy in particular. He walked down the stairs a skip ahead of her.

"Did anyone ever tell you your dad is as hard to reason with as a two-headed bull?"

His blue eyes widened, then he clamped a hand over his mouth. She wondered what had happened to make a kid hold his laughter inside as if afraid to share it with the world. Her heart took a tumble.

There was one thing about being a lonely-only; she'd turned to reading to fill the hours—a habit she still had. One book she'd read recently was about a doctor who worked with autistic children. He'd used play therapy to draw the children out. She decided she'd include J.J. in her activities.

"Could you eat a snowman pancake if I made one?" she asked, putting on her bright face.

He nodded. His smile widened.

She glanced outside. The sun was shining. The snow had melted in the clearings although it clung tenaciously to the cool shade of the forests. Spring was creeping in. And in the paddock, working with a colt on a lunge line, was her newly acquired husband.

A lump formed in her throat. He looked handsome and virile and so very capable as he put the colt through its paces. Dawn was astride a big roan gelding on the gravel road. She halted the gelding and watched Hunter.

Celia heard her new sister-in-law call out, but couldn't make out the words. Hunter released the colt and climbed onto the fence. He shook his head, glanced at the ranch house, then answered something Dawn said before she nudged the gelding and took off at a gentle canter.

The lump grew two sizes. Celia forced it down, then went about preparing pancakes for her small family. When she had J.J. seated with his "snowman," she went to the door and called to Hunter.

For a minute she didn't think he was going to heed her, but then he ambled toward the house, stopping to talk briefly to Tom who appeared at the stable door.

"Would you like to join us for breakfast?" she asked when he entered the kitchen.

He looked at her, at the table set with the stoneware dishes glazed with a pretty floral edge, then at J.J., who had stopped smiling and eating and was watching his father with eyes too old for his young age.

She realized the boy was wary of his father—not afraid, but not at ease, either. She glanced at Hunter. He looked like the model for the original Great Stone Face.

"I have to go to town this morning and get my clothes and car so I can get settled in this week. Does J.J. go to preschool?"

"No."

"Hmm. Does he stay with you during the day?"

Hunter gave her a sharp glance at the disapproving tone. "Sometimes, or with Dawn or his grandmother. Hazel lives at the house down the road. He'll go to church with her this morning while we go to town."

"I see." She busied herself at the stove. When she returned to the table with her plate, she noticed Hunter had waited for her before eating.

Her tough rancher husband was innately polite. He could be kind when he chose. And she knew he loved his son.

While she'd taken four child-psychology classes at

university, she understood J.J. instinctively. She saw herself in the child and knew he needed to feel wanted.

She would speak to Hunter about his son, but she'd give him some time to get used to having her around first. In the meantime, she would set a good example.

Yes, that was a better plan. Married two days and already thinking of confronting her husband over the way he was raising his son was probably not a good idea. She would most likely pass out from terror before she could tell him what he needed to do.

"What's funny?" he asked, breaking into the mental scenario of her in a dead faint and Tom and the cowboys blaming Hunter for roaring at her.

"I'll tell you later." She glanced at J.J. and found him watching her with his usual solemn stare. She winked at the child and smiled as if they had a big secret. "J.J. brought me a cracker this morning. It made me feel ever so much better. Wasn't that thoughtful?"

Hunter's eyes narrowed. After a couple of seconds, he grunted an agreement.

Oh, yes, they were definitely going to have to have some changes—when she felt a bit more comfortable as the woman of the house...and when her husband had learned to accept her in that role.

Chapter Seven

"I'd like to tour the ranch," Celia, as bright as a sunbeam in a yellow outfit, announced on Wednesday.

"You ride?" Hunter asked, surprised. He'd assumed that his town-bred wife didn't know much about ranch life.

"Ride? On a horse? No. They scare me to death."

"Then how're you going to tour the ranch?"

"I meant the immediate vicinity."

"I have a sick cow I need to treat. You can come down to the barn, I guess." He had a feeling that was a bad idea, but he didn't know exactly what to do with her. "By the way, Tom's going to take over cooking for the men."

"Oh." Distress flashed in her eyes before that stubborn smile popped up on her face. "I don't mind doing it. Didn't they like the simpler things—the soup and the pot roast? The crown roast was in your freezer," she ended in defense of the fancy meal she'd prepared the first night.

"Mom liked to fix something fancy for company once in a while. In summer, we grill burgers and steaks a lot."

"I see."

He felt like a curmudgeon who'd taken a toy from a child. He tried a lighter note. "Look, I don't expect you to slave for a bunch of cowboys. I know you modern women don't believe in it."

"I like to cook."

"All right. I'll tell Tom you'll do it."

"I might not have time when school starts back."

He took a deep breath. "Fine. We'll let him handle it."

"Maybe he and I could take turns." She propped her chin on her hands while she thought this over, her expression as earnest as if they were working out world peace.

"Why don't you talk to Tom? You and he can work it out." He couldn't keep his exasperation from coming through.

Glancing over at J.J., he noted the boy's eyes on him. J.J. looked down at his plate, his mouth crimped in at the corners. Hunter got the distinct impression his son didn't like the way he'd spoken to Celia. He felt compelled to apologize. For his son's sake.

"Uh, look, I didn't mean to sound harsh—"

"Why not?" she asked equably. "That's the way you feel. You don't want me here. Perhaps we should have thought about this marriage a while longer—"

"It's nearly three months too late for that." His jaw went stiff as the irritation built. "The time to think was on New Year's Eve."

A hot flush hit her cheeks. "I know." She looked young and vulnerable for a second. Her smile wobbled, but held.

He met J.J.'s eyes and looked away, feeling guilty for his prickly temper. "Let's go to the barn."

They put on jackets. Celia was the first out the door. She shrank back when the Lab bounded up to them.

"Relax. The Lab is J.J.'s dog. He won't hurt you."

"I remember him from when I was here before. He stayed right on my heels when I went to my car."

"That's because you were running. He thought you were playing with him. You nearly caught his nose in the car door when you slammed it."

J.J. petted the frisky dog, which became quiet under the boy's touch.

"What's his name?"

"He doesn't have one."

She looked shocked. "All pets have names."

"We call him 'the Lab.'"

"That's terrible."

Hunter refrained from cursing.

J.J. reached for her hand and guided it to the dog's head. Hunter watched as his son introduced his pet to the new member of the household. Celia tentatively scratched the dog's ears. The Lab sighed in ecstasy. She and J.J. smiled at each other.

"How about Blackie?" she asked the boy. "He's certainly black all over."

J.J. shook his head.

"Okay. I read a book once about a dog. His name was Lad. Do you like that?"

J.J. shook his head.

"How about Midnight? Bingo? Killer?"

J.J.'s grin widened with each suggestion.

"I know. Lab."

His son nodded.

"Lab, it is," she agreed. The dog jumped around her, managing to lick her face a couple of times. "Oh, yuck, germs." She laughed and petted the mutt.

"Come on," Hunter snapped. "I haven't got all day. I have a sick cow to tend."

"What's wrong with her?" Celia asked as she, J.J. and the Lab fell into step alongside him.

"She has an udder infection."

His new wife looked alarmed at this news. "Poor thing," she murmured, crossing her arms over her chest.

Her breasts bunched up, swelling above the press of her arms into enticing mounds against the peach shirt. From the open V of her jacket and shirt lapels, he could see the paleness of her skin. A feeling that he'd once explored the smooth contours of those very feminine curves came to him.

According to her, he'd explored all of her thoroughly.

The surge of need that racked through him was so strong he nearly groaned aloud. Anger at himself, at her, at life, added to the sense of desperation that followed the need.

He cursed long and silently on the walk to the barn. Inside, the sick cow started a racket that was picked up by a couple of orphaned calves he was hand-feeding.

"Watch it," he warned. "We brought some beeves through here this morning. We haven't had time to muck out the place yet." He pointed out a cow pile so the town girl would know exactly what he was talking about.

She stepped around the droppings and watched while he selected a syringe. "Do you know how to give a shot?" There was definitely admiration in her tone.

"All ranchers do."

"Did April?"

"Yes."

J.J. and the Lab wandered over to a runt calf's stall. He looked a question at Hunter.

"I'll fix the milk buckets," Hunter said. He laid the syringe aside and prepared the powdered-milk solution for the calves. He handed one bucket to J.J., and one to his wife. "You think you can give this to one of the calves?"

"Sure."

"J.J. can show you how."

He watched while she followed J.J. to the stalls. The calves stuck their heads out the slats and latched on to the nipples that protruded out the side of the buckets. Celia laughed as if this was a thrilling experience. She looked almost as young as his son.

Instead of getting on with his work, he stood there and watched the other two at their task. Celia tentatively patted the calf's horn buds, then searched out their shape with her fingertip in the fringe of longer hair on the animal's topknot. The calf eyed her but kept sucking.

"Just hang the bucket on that nail when he's through," Hunter advised.

"Right." She looked as serious as a doctor doing brain surgery.

Shaking his head, Hunter prepared the syringe and went into the stall with the sick cow. "Easy, girl, easy, now."

Kneeling, he cleaned her udder and squirted a drop of medicine out of the needle.

"Where are you going to give her the shot?" Celia asked, leaning over the top railing—an act that caused her breasts to bunch again.

His mouth went dry. "In the teat."

A look of horror passed over her face. "Her... her... In her..."

"Teat. That's right. Try not to faint."

She gave him an indignant glare. "I won't."

Just as he was about to plunge the needle in, Celia's screech made him jerk. He nearly stuck the shot into his own hand. "What the hell?" he snarled.

Rising, he stared at his wife as she drew back in panic. Her shirt was stretched out to one side. She let out another screech. The sick cow jostled around and stepped on his foot. He cursed again and pushed the animal aside.

Hurriedly exiting the stall, he saw what the problem was. The yearling in the next pen had thought he should get some breakfast, too. He'd sucked the tail of Celia's shirt into his mouth and was working on getting all of it. As Celia drew back, the yearling held on and yanked the other way. Since the animal weighed three times what she did, the yearling was winning the tug-of-war.

J.J. rushed over. The Lab barked and sank down, his head between his front paws, his hind end in the air, tail wagging furiously, ready for a new, exciting game.

Before Hunter could act, J.J. gave the yearling a smart rap on the nose. The young bull bellowed and let go of Celia's shirt. She flew backward and landed with a distinct splat.

Another screech followed, much different from the first two. "Oh. Oh. Oh," she said with a rising inflection.

She looked so comical—so horrified and indignant—he laughed out loud. Then he heard a strange sound, one he hadn't heard in a long time. He whipped his head around.

J.J. had a hand pressed over his mouth. His shoulders shook. J.J. was laughing.

The boy went to Celia and held out his hand. He kept the other clamped over his lips, holding the laughter in as best he could. Celia grinned up at him, then took the offer of a hand and let him help her up.

She viewed her backside and wrinkled her nose. "Phewey," she said.

J.J. laughed some more. Aloud.

She paused and looked at the boy, then darted an astonished glance his way.

Hunter's grin faded. From inside, from that dark, cold, soulless place, something strange happened. For a second, light blazed inside him, blinding him.

Turning from the smile Celia beamed on him, he fumbled his way into the stall and gave the cow her shot. She bellowed. The yearling joined in, then the calves.

When he came out, Celia was gone. He saw her and J.J. and the dog heading toward the house. He stored the medicine in the first-aid kit and put it away. His hands trembled.

His son's laughter echoed in his ears, drowning the racket from the cattle. There had been times in the past when he would have given his right arm to hear that sound.

He stared at Celia's retreating form. This woman, this wife he didn't want, who didn't belong on the ranch, had made him and his son laugh. He looked around the empty barn and felt the backwash of loneliness pour over his soul.

Celia put the vacuum cleaner in the hall closet and straightened. Pressing both hands into the small of her back, she massaged the stiffness from achy muscles. Glancing around the great room, she sighed in satisfaction.

The house was shining. She'd vacuumed ceilings and corners and furniture this past week. She'd opened the drapes and left them that way, then she'd cleaned the windows. Freshly washed sheers hung from the rods. Although she'd felt like an interloper, she'd done the same in the master suite and in the study, which was Mrs. McLean's bedroom.

After washing clothes yesterday, she'd straightened first J.J.'s room, then Hunter's, arranging underwear and socks and T-shirts into drawers, and separating suits, pants and shirts in the closet until every item was in order.

Hunter hadn't said a word about her cleaning efforts. Or maybe he considered it meddling.

In the afternoon, she and J.J. had gone to town and brought her plants back to the ranch. Now ivy and variegated philodendron hung from baskets while the kitchen windowsill bloomed with tiny pots of her favorite herbs. Three earthenware jars sported a blaze of spring color with daisies and tulips and greenery— one in the kitchen and two in the great room.

J.J. had chosen a rubber plant for his room from the local garden store. She'd selected a ficus for the great room and a jade plant for the kitchen. The store had delivered them this morning.

Hunter had frowned and left the house without a word while she directed the placement of the plants. He had grown noticeably cooler toward her this past week. To be in the room with him was like standing next to a glacier.

She went into the kitchen where bread was baking in a machine especially for that purpose. She'd found it in the back corner of the pantry and decided to try it. The entire house smelled delicious.

Hunter had taken J.J. with him to the stable to work with the foals and new calves that morning, then Dawn had stopped by to tell her J.J. was going to town with her.

To Celia's surprise, the child had chosen to stay with her most of the week. J.J. was a wonderful worker with a great deal of discipline for a three-year-old. The more she was around him, the more she liked him.

They were establishing a rapport and a routine. She'd started reading to him each afternoon at nap time. After the mishap in the barn, he'd climbed into her lap for the story and had done so each day since. His trust and acceptance touched her heart. If only his father could be won...

Pouring a cup of coffee, she decided she really needed to talk to Hunter about his dealings with his son. Except she didn't think he wanted to hear anything from her.

Instead of smoothing out, their relationship seemed to be intensifying into solid dislike on his part. On hers, she wasn't sure what she felt. Occasionally, while working around the house or taking a walk or having coffee with Dawn, she would grow hopeful about the marriage.

When she was around Hunter, however, her hopes died a swift death. He was polite, but it was obvious he tolerated her only because he felt he had to. At times, the bleakness in his eyes almost made her cry.

But she didn't. She'd learned long ago not to let another's unhappiness daunt her. She took her pleasures from simple things—a favorite melody, a clean, well-ordered home, the loveliness of flowers.

The bread maker dinged.

She removed the perfectly browned loaf and laid it on a cooling rack. Unable to resist, she cut an end off and slathered it with margarine and the jam she'd made last July from blackberries she'd picked herself. She sat down and bit into the slice. Umm, delicious!

The kitchen door opened. Hunter entered. He stopped abruptly. His gaze flew to the bread machine, then to her.

"Where did you get that?" he demanded.

This sounded like one of those trick questions she was never sure how to answer. "In the pantry?"

She hated the uncertainty conveyed by that rise at the end, making her answer a question, as if she had to ask him if it was okay for her to use the darned thing.

"I assumed it would be okay to try it. I mean, it looked new and it seemed to work fine, so I thought it might be fun to make bread. I never have before—"

"It's okay," he said, cutting off her disjoined explanation. He poured a cup of coffee.

"Would you like some? It's hot and very good. I have homemade jam, too." She leaped to her feet.

"No, thanks." His voice was like a growl from the jagged bowels of the earth.

She sat down, knowing she'd done something wrong, but she wasn't sure what. An idea came to her. "Was the bread maker a wedding gift to you and April?"

From her reading, she knew it was better to get his past relationship out in the open. Until Hunter accepted her as his wife, their marriage didn't have a chance.

"No. It was a Christmas present. From me." He stared at the pots of herbs on the windowsill as if angry about them.

"Do you like the plants?" she asked, her tone the color of a sunbeam in contrast to his dark one. "I brought them from my house— Oh, that reminds me. The fifth-grade teacher just got married and she and her husband are interested in renting the place. Do you think that's a good idea?"

He shrugged.

She liked the idea of having a small-but-steady income of her own. That way, she could leave her modest investments intact and let them grow. Perhaps she could stay at home with the baby next year and yet have money coming in. She and Hunter hadn't discussed finances.

"Well, I think I might." She finished her snack in silence and put the plate in the dishwasher. She hesitated beside the bread maker. "Would you rather I put this away and not use it?"

"It's all right."

By which she took him to mean it was okay to use it. The joy had gone out of the idea of baking her own bread, though. She'd felt sort of like a pioneer woman while she'd measured the ingredients, even if a machine was doing the mixing and kneading and baking, but still, it had been fun.

Leaning against the counter, she watched her husband. He was withdrawn, as he'd been all week, his mood dark and introspective. She'd rather cut her tongue out than ask him to talk to her, but the truth was she was lonely—more so than she'd ever been in her little two-bedroom house with its five acres of pine trees by the lake.

"Uh," she said to catch his attention rather than calling him by name. When he looked up, she continued, "Some friends and I usually have dinner out on Friday. I thought I'd go into town tonight." She got the last out in a rush, but at least it didn't end in a question as if she were asking permission.

"No," he said as if she had.

Her head snapped up at his uncompromising stare.

PLAY
RUN FOR THE ROSES

...and you
can get

FREE BOOKS and a FREE GIFT!

Turn the page and let the race begin!

PLAY

RUN
FOR THE
ROSES

and get
THREE FREE GIFTS!

HOW TO PLAY:

1. With a coin, carefully scratch off the silver box at the right. Then check the claim chart to see what we have for you — **FREE BOOKS** and a **FREE GIFT**—**ALL YOURS FREE!**

2. Send back the card and you'll receive two brand-new Silhouette Special Edition® novels. These books have a cover price of $4.25 each, but they are yours to keep absolutely free.

3. There's no catch. You're under no obligation to buy anything. We charge nothing — ZERO — for your first shipment. And you don't have to make any minimum number of purchases — not even one!

4. The fact is, thousands of readers enjoy receiving books by mail from the Silhouette Reader Service™. They like the convenience of home delivery...they like getting the best new novels months before they're available in stores...and they love our discount prices!

5. We hope that after receiving your free books you'll want to remain a subscriber. But the choice is yours — to continue or cancel, any time at all! So why not take us up on our invitation, with no risk of any kind. You'll be glad you did!

This surprise mystery gift
Will be yours **FREE** –
When you play
RUN for the ROSES

The Silhouette Reader Service™ — Here's how it works:

If offer card is missing write to: Silhouette Reader Service, 3010 Walden Ave., P.O. Box 1867, Buffalo NY 14240-1867

BUSINESS REPLY MAIL
FIRST-CLASS MAIL   PERMIT NO. 717   BUFFALO, NY

POSTAGE WILL BE PAID BY ADDRESSEE

SILHOUETTE READER SERVICE
3010 WALDEN AVE
PO BOX 1867
BUFFALO NY 14240-9952

NO POSTAGE
NECESSARY
IF MAILED
IN THE
UNITED STATES

She met his eyes. "I'm expected. I told Terri I'd be there."

"The roads will be icy tonight. The warm weather has caused a lot of snow to melt. The roads are wet. They'll ice over when the sun goes down and the temperature drops."

He pushed his chair back and headed outside, the door closing softly but with a decisive click behind him.

"And that's that," she said to the empty room.

Hearing a car on the road, she went to the door. Dawn and J.J. were back from town. She waved to Dawn and waited for J.J. to come inside. Lab dashed up from the stable for a pat on the head, then raced off.

Celia had an idea. "Hi, how would you like to go into town this afternoon and spend the night at my place?"

J.J. looked worried as he thought it over, then nodded.

Her heart went out to him—this serious little boy who stayed carefully within himself. "We'll leave a note for your father," she promised.

She wrote Hunter a note and stuck it on the fridge with a magnet. J.J. picked out his favorite Batman pajamas and a change of clothing and put them in a knapsack. She did the same. "Toothbrush," she reminded. He ran to get his.

Later, after letting him explore her small house and giving him the guest bedroom, they did some shopping and went to a movie. She discovered it was J.J.'s first time at the theater. They had popcorn and sodas.

On the way home, she drove past the community

cemetery. She pulled in, determined to carry out another idea she'd had earlier. She parked and invited J.J. to come with her.

At the McLean plot, she pointed out his grandfather's grave and read the headstone to him. J.J. pointed to another one. She told him who each person was and their relationship to him. Finally, she stopped beside his mother's stone.

"April Ann McLean," she read. She outlined the letters with her finger. "April was your mother. Did you know that?"

He shook his head.

"I knew her all my life. I was born here in town. She was born in the house where your Grandma Ericson lives, but we went to the same church and were in school together."

Celia sat down on the granite ledge that formed the base of the stone. J.J. hesitated, then joined her, sitting close so that they touched each other.

"Would you like to know about your mother?"

He nodded.

"She was beautiful. Have you seen a picture? No? I saw an album at the ranch. We'll look at it tomorrow. Your mommy was tall and blond and blue-eyed like Aunt Dawn and she could ride any horse in the world, she was that good. As good as your father and uncle."

For an hour, she told him stories of his mother.

"When you were born, she was so happy. I went to visit her at the hospital. She was nursing you. Did you know you nursed from her just like the calves nurse from the cows?"

He looked amazed.

"You did. She held you right against her heart and fed you. She loved you so much, so very, very much. She was so glad to have you. She said you were the most beautiful baby in the world."

J.J. looked doubtful.

"Honest." Celia crossed her heart. "And you were the smartest baby, too. You walked before you were a year old and you knew exactly where your food was stored in the pantry. Your mom said you could pick out what you wanted to eat by looking at the pictures on the jars. Pretty sharp for a kid, huh?"

He looked shyly pleased.

"April told everyone how smart you were. I was really impressed." She smiled at J.J. so he'd know how special he was, and she was rewarded with a smile from him.

Her heart ached when she looked into his eyes and saw his uncertainty. On impulse, she lifted him into her lap and hugged and kissed him. He was a wiry little boy, his arms and legs stick thin, but strong. He wrapped his arms around her neck and squeezed with surprising strength.

When she felt his mouth touch her cheek, her heart filled with the most painful overflow of love she'd ever experienced. "I love you, too," she whispered, pressing her face into his neck and giving him lots of kisses.

"Mmm," he said.

She sat very still, then tears filled her eyes. It was a moment before she could speak. "Let's go join the gals for dinner, shall we?"

Hunter stopped with one foot on the patio step. The light was on in the kitchen, but he didn't see anyone inside. The rest of the house was dark. A strange feeling grabbed his insides as he went in.

The house was empty.

He could sense it the way animals could sense an approaching storm. He glanced around at the flowers, the pots of herbs, the magazines with their colorful covers stacked in a basket on the floor.

The whole house was different. Brighter. Friendlier. Welcoming. As it had once been.

Pain, sharp as volcanic glass, cut at feelings he'd buried almost three years ago. He blocked out the light and the possibilities of the future as epitomized by the warmth of the house. He'd never find that wild joy again, the smug confidence that he held all he loved safely in his hands. Life had taught him a bitter lesson. It didn't need repeating.

Grimly he checked the premises. Where the hell were Celia and J.J.? He was tired. He wanted to shower, then eat. He didn't want a hassle.

A sheet of paper from his son's tablet caught his eye. He walked over and read it. Dinner was in the oven, the fresh bread in the plastic bag on the counter. Cookies were in the jar. Celia and J.J. were spending the night in town.

Irritation swept through him. He'd told her not to go to town. The roads would be dangerous. He read the note again. Okay, so she was staying at her place. Fine.

While he showered and changed, he argued with himself about going to town and checking on them. Returning to the kitchen, he removed a huge pot of beef stew from the oven and put the bread on the oak table. The cowboys came in and served themselves.

"Sure miss that sunny smile," Tom remarked, glancing at the empty chair where Celia usually sat. "Don't it beat all how a little gal like that can make such a big difference."

"Are you going to eat or soliloquize?" Hunter snapped.

"Do what? Is that a word? Jason, you been going to college and all. You ever heard 'soliloquize'?"

Jason grinned and nodded.

"Where are the missus and the boy?" Tom asked.

Hunter shook his head. The old geezer was determined to drive him nuts. "They're spending the night in town. Do you want the number so you can call and hear her voice before you go to sleep?"

"Naw, I'll just imagine what she sounds like—so chipper and friendly, like. Not like some I could mention."

Pete snorted and choked on a piece of bread while Rick and Jason hid their smiles behind their hands.

After the men left, the house settled back into silence. Hunter cleared the kitchen, then slumped in front of the television. His mind wasn't on world problems. He thought of the roads. It would be like Celia to decide to return to the ranch for some reason.

She'd fluttered in and out all week, running to town, to her house, back to the ranch, rearranging everything in the place—well, closets and things. It had taken him ten minutes to find his underwear neatly laid out in a drawer the other day. He'd been leaving the laundry in the basket and rooting through it for things he needed.

He glanced out the window. The thermometer hovered a hair above freezing now that night had fallen. Maybe he'd better go into town. No, he hadn't been invited.

Scowling, he prowled the house. From the kitchen, he heard the sound of the pet door in the garage opening. The Lab had found it too frosty to stay outside tonight. He'd come in from the cold.

His son loved the animal, but it hadn't brought the boy out of his silent ways. Celia had. Her pratfall had made him and his son laugh. He smiled, remembering it.

The amusement disappeared under the onslaught of images that raced through his mind—laughter and low, sexy murmurs; hands reaching out to him, pulling him close; then the incredible warmth as he, too, came in out of the cold....

Chapter Eight

"I want to talk to you about something. About J.J.," Celia added at Hunter's quizzical glance as he stopped with his hand on the doorknob.

She had decided this was as good a time as any to broach the grouchy, uh, lion in his den, so to speak. J.J. was playing with Lab in the yard, so she and Hunter had the house to themselves.

"What about him?"

"Well, uh, I want you to smile at him more."

Celia groaned at her lack of finesse. Telling Hunter McLean what he was doing wrong in raising his son was about as smart as smacking a gorilla in the face. She smiled brightly to give him an idea of what she meant.

"What?" he retorted, his dark brows drawing closer.

She was aware of his restless gaze running over her and wondered if her shorts were too short when he stared at her legs. Heat swept through her, and she nearly forgot what she was saying. Determined to stick to her guns, she continued, "I want you to give him big, welcoming smiles."

His attention shifted to her face, but not before she saw the blaze of hunger in his eyes.

"A child needs to know he's wanted," she added in a rush, sure she'd imagined the sensual need. His expression had altered to a listening attitude. "Did you ever notice how women smile and coo at infants? And the way their eyebrows go up and their eyes open real wide?"

She exaggerated the movements so he'd understand. Until she caught a glimpse of her reflection in the windowpane—mouth wide, eyebrows flashing in and out of her bangs like woolly worms with the hiccups.

"Well, you get the idea," she finished, maintaining her equilibrium with an effort as his eyes flicked over her again. Maybe she hadn't imagined the flames....

Hunter jammed his hands into his pockets and took up a stance with his legs apart.

Well, nobody liked being told they were doing wrong.... Well, not exactly wrong, just not quite right. Besides, the lecture wasn't just for J.J.'s sake. Hunter needed to open up and let his feelings out. Inside, he still grieved for his lost love.

She swallowed the knot in her throat. "I think that's because women instinctively know how to make a child feel loved. That look tells the child he's the center of their world, that he has merit just by *being*.''

Pausing, she gazed at Hunter to see if he was getting any of this. He nodded, his lips crimped so tightly, she could see muscles bunching at the corners of his mouth. Oh, dear, he looked really angry.

She tried to explain it better. ''It's important to a child—not just any child, of course—but *your* child…because his world revolves around you, you know, until he grows up and finds someone…. Well, that's years away.'' She swallowed as the darkness gathered like a rain cloud in his eyes. ''It's important that J.J. should know you want him.''

Finished, breathless, she waited for Hunter's reaction. It wasn't long in coming.

''Of course, I want him!'' he thundered. ''He's my son. I'm with him a good part of every day, less now that you're taking him to nursery school, but I still see him more than men who work in offices in town.''

''Yes, it's very good of you to let him attend Tiny Tots play school these last two months of the school year,'' she said to soothe his ruffled feathers. ''He needed to be around other children—'' She broke off at the obvious clenching of his jaw.

Actually, he'd been quite open to her suggestion. He even let her take J.J. with her to kindergarten the other two mornings of the week. J.J. had been going with her for a month now, and she was proud of the headway she'd made with her stepson.

Although she'd never heard him talk, he joined the other children in their games now. At first he'd only watched them while they played and acted out songs and stories. Sometimes he moved his mouth, and she wondered if he was singing.

That was why she had wanted to speak to Hunter today. She thought they were on the cusp of a break-through with J.J.

"But you don't smile," she said. "You need to have fun with him, laugh with him, but most of all, just smile, as if each time you see him your world is made right by the fact that he's in it."

And for a second, she envisioned such a smile turned on her—welcoming, loving....

He remained so impassive she wasn't sure he was listening to her message at all.

She laid her hand on his arm. "Please, can you do that? Would you try it for a while?"

He stared at her hand until she grew self-conscious and removed it. Finally he gazed into her eyes. "Yes," he said in a harsh, raspy tone that sent shivers up her spine. "I can do that." He walked out, closing the door behind him with an almost-eerie quietness.

Even the house seemed to sigh as the tension seeped out of the room. Well, at least he hadn't snapped her head off for meddling in his life. She sank down in a chair until her nerves calmed, then she went back to making pies for supper.

Things were going pretty well at the ranch. She and Tom had agreed on a schedule that worked well for the meals.

She cooked Monday through Thursday, making enough for leftovers for the weekend. The grizzled ranch hand prepared for Saturday and the noon meals, mostly sandwiches unless she put on a stew or pot roast before she and J.J. left for school. On Friday night and Sunday, the men were on their own.

She'd rented the cottage in town to a fifth-grade teacher and her husband, so that was taken care of.

Each afternoon, while J.J. took a nap, she did one chore in the house—dusting or laundry or general cleaning.

She was growing more accustomed to being Hunter's wife. The teachers and the townspeople were getting used to it, too, although she knew there had been a lot of speculation, especially with Hunter demanding marriage in the restaurant, not caring who heard their quarrel over it.

For the first week, each time she'd entered the teachers' lounge, there had been a profound pause, then a rush of conversation to cover it. She'd certainly come to understand her mother's resentment of small-town life.

Finished with the baking now, she went in search of paint to spruce up the back door. She'd washed woodwork each afternoon that week. The house was shining clean. Hunter couldn't say she didn't do a good job there.

Feeling somewhat sanctimonious about her hard work, she considered going down to the storage shed next to the barn. She'd seen paint on one of the shelves while searching out a spade for the flowers she and J.J. and Tom had planted around the house and down one side of the barn.

However, Hunter had ordered her not to go anywhere on the ranch alone. On her first adventure away from the house, she'd cut through a pretty meadow while taking fresh-baked brownies to Hunter and the men where they'd been working on fences in a nearby pasture.

All the prize breeding stock had gotten out.

Well, how was she to have known the silver mare belonging to Dawn could open gates, and that was why the little twist of wire was around the first gate she'd gone through?

Dawn's mare had followed along behind her, opening gates as fast as she closed them all along the way. She hadn't realized it until one of the men yelled and she'd seen the new bull and the heifers take off down the ranch road for parts unknown.

It had taken three days to find and herd them back to their proper place. Hunter hadn't yelled at her. He'd simply suggested she stick close to the house in the future.

On her second excursion, she'd come upon two of the cowboys with a young mare. They'd tied a handkerchief around her nose and a rope around her feet so she couldn't bite or kick, then they'd let another horse in with her. The other horse had screamed and nipped at her and chased her around the paddock until she stood trembling in terror.

The whole episode had been shocking to Celia. She'd tried to fight off the bigger horse with a broom...until Hunter had yanked her out of the paddock and up to the house where he'd explained in no uncertain terms that she wasn't to interfere with the breeding program.

"You mean...you tied her up to let that big brute...have his way with her? But he was hurting her—"

"No, he wasn't. He's a gentle stallion."

She'd stared at Hunter, aghast. "He wasn't gentle. She was whinnying and trying to get away—"

"That's the way horses do," he'd said, tight-lipped with anger. He'd stalked over to the door. "You embarrassed the hell out of the men. From now on, don't leave the house without my permission."

"How am I going to get to school?" she'd asked, not to be facetious, but because she was surprised and upset and tended to say the first thing that popped into her head.

He'd stopped at the door and given her a look that sizzled over her until she felt like a burned match. "Don't go anywhere on the *ranch* without me." Then he'd left.

She looked at the kitchen door, at the clear sky. The weather was perfect. And all she needed was a little paint. No need to bother Hunter about that. One quick trip to the shed and back. He'd never know she'd been in the place....

The shed door creaked pleasantly when she opened it. She peered around. Yes, there were several paint cans lined up in a neat row on the top shelf.

She read the names of the colors. Shadow White Exterior Enamel, Satin Finish. That sounded as if it was exactly what she was looking for. Now she only had to reach it.

Peering at the rickety shelves, she decided they might not take her weight. Ah. She grabbed a garden rake propped in the corner and flipped it over, knocking it against the low ceiling as she did.

Suddenly a buzz whirled around her head. She stared in surprise as several wasps flew in a tight circle only inches from her nose. One landed on her bangs. She could see it crawling around in a circle. Its stinger arced downward.

She let out a shriek and batted at them.

The nest, which had been hanging from the ceiling, now clung precariously to the upended rake. It swung wildly to and fro. More wasps appeared.

"Ai-i-i-i." She screamed bloody murder and ran.

She fell out the door when Hunter yanked it open from the outside at the same time she pushed from the inside.

"What's wrong?" he demanded, grabbing her arm.

"Wa-wasps!" she gasped, clinging to his powerful shoulders. She didn't have to explain further. One of them dive-bombed her at that moment.

He swatted her with his hat, knocking the wasp off with the brim, and thrust her behind him.

"Run!" he ordered, holding the angry beasts off with mighty swings of his arm.

She dashed for the house as hard as she could go. A few seconds later, Hunter caught up with her. Grabbing J.J. from the patio steps, he propelled them along even faster.

They burst through the kitchen door. He slammed it behind them and leaned against it, breathing hard for about ten breaths. She sank into a chair, gasping and holding her side with one hand, her burning cheek with the other. She was almost afraid to look at him.

He didn't appear furious, she saw when she screwed up her courage and glanced his way. J.J. stood to one side, his gaze switching from one to the other.

"I haven't had to outrun a bunch of angry hornets

since I was twelve and threw rocks at them," Hunter announced.

Was that laughter tripping through his voice? She wasn't sure. At any rate, her cheek hurt terribly. "I hit the nest with the rake and knocked it off the ceiling."

"What were you doing in the shed?" His eyes gleamed as they roamed over her, stopping at her legs as they often did. He confused her with his intense perusals.

"Well, I was going to paint the back door. Before the spring rains. I remembered seeing some paint...." Her voice trailed off.

"You should have told me you wanted the paint earlier this afternoon. I'd have gotten it for you."

"I didn't think—" Not a good thing to say, she realized, seeing his sardonic grin. "I'm sorry."

She waited for the dressing-down she deserved and gingerly explored the stung place. Her whole cheek felt on fire. It was swelling, too.

J.J. touched her arm and pointed toward her face.

Hunter pulled her hand away. With an exclamation, he grabbed a paper towel and an ice cube from the freezer. "Put that on your cheek."

Holding her free arm, he led her down the hall and into the master suite. She skipped along and tried to keep the ice cube on her face. Its cool wetness helped.

The master bathroom was spacious. It had a whirlpool tub and a separate shower. Twin sinks lined one wall. The door to the walk-in closet was open.

"There's always allergy medicine in the barn and stable and in this cabinet," he informed her. "A rancher runs into all kinds of stinging things."

After opening a tube of allergy ointment, he dabbed her cheek liberally with the medication. She immediately felt a soothing sensation. He gave her two pills, then threw three of them into his own mouth. He filled a glass with water and held it out to her.

"Are these okay to take?" she asked.

"Yes, April used this type. It won't hurt the baby."

She nodded and swallowed the pills. He let her drink first, then he finished the water in the glass.

"Were you stung?" she asked, feeling terribly guilty. "Let me see. I'll make sure the stinger is out and put the medicine on for you."

"I'm okay. Use this when you need it." He handed the tube of medicine to her. "The pills make you sleepy, so don't do anything for the rest of the afternoon. I'll see about someone keeping J.J. You rest."

"Okay." Eyes smarting with sudden tears at his kindness, she followed him to the living room.

J.J. climbed up beside her in their favorite chair.

She managed a smile to reassure him that she was fine. He patted her arm and snuggled close. Hunter watched them for a few seconds, his mood unreadable, then left.

Her nerves calmed. J.J. looked at a storybook while she dozed. Mrs. Ericson came to the house an hour later.

"Hunter told me what happened. I'll keep J.J. tonight. You take care of yourself," the older woman advised. She shook her head at Celia's swollen face, then collected her grandson's pajamas and toothbrush.

J.J. gave her a kiss on her good cheek before he left.

Alone, Celia hit the button that popped the footrest

out and pulled a comforter over herself. She would have cried except it hurt too much to move her face. Placing a hand on her tummy, which now felt as if she'd swallowed a grapefruit, she went to sleep worried about the effect of the bee venom on the baby.

She woke with a start two hours later. Looking at the shadows outside, she saw it was twilight.

Her cheek felt grotesque, hot and tight and plumped up. Thank goodness she had the weekend to recover. No one would see her, except her husband. She stared at him in surprise.

Hunter was lying on the sofa. He'd shucked his shirt and the T-shirt he usually wore. She saw a red welt where he'd been stung. She removed the cap from the ointment, rubbed some more on her cheek, which no longer burned, then knelt on the floor. He jumped when she touched him.

"Hold still. There's a spot on the back of your neck. And your shoulder. Oh, and here."

She covered each sting as she discovered it—six of them altogether. Guilt tore at her. He'd been hurt because of her carelessness.

"That feels better," he murmured when she treated the last welt on his side above his jeans.

She laid the ointment on the coffee table. "I'm so sorry. I wanted to get a can of paint off the top shelf. I was going to use the rake because I couldn't reach it—"

He laid a finger over her stumbling apology. "I should have gotten rid of them. I knew they were there."

"We were lucky they didn't come after us."

"They did. We outran them." To her surprise, he

lightly brushed his fingers over her swollen cheek. "Were you on a track team?"

"No. I wasn't very athletic in school. I guess I was a geek. I was sort of quiet."

Tingles rushed over her as he continued to stroke her cheek, then her lips, very, very gently. The bare expanse of his chest beckoned her to rest her head there. She thought of sleeping curled up next to him.

She'd never in her life woken with a man in her bed. It sounded...interesting.

Those first nights at the ranch had been difficult. The darkness had been blacker than in town where streetlights beamed from every corner. During two storms, the lightning had seemed much closer to the house than at her cozy cottage in town. She'd had trouble falling asleep. It would have been nice to have someone to cuddle with.

She still woke up in the middle of the night at times, not sure what was bothering her. Once it had been a wild chorus of coyotes—or maybe wolves— that had frightened her. She'd lain in bed, alone and afraid....

Not that she would ever admit her fears to Hunter. He already knew she wasn't cut out to be a rancher's wife.

"Would you like me to put ice on your spots?" she asked.

"It isn't necessary. I've been stung before. It really doesn't bother me all that much."

"Oh."

Against her hip, his warmth permeated her jeans. A buzz hummed along her nerves. His hand dropped to her shoulder. He caressed her neck and collarbone.

She felt woozy and disoriented, as if she'd woken in a different place than where she'd gone to sleep.

"This isn't Kansas," she murmured, smiling a little, even though it hurt.

She'd spun such dreams about this man when she'd been a teenager. She'd even pretended she was the bride when she'd attended his wedding years later. Such longing she'd felt!

Tears filled her throat. She'd never been a crybaby, but lately that had been all she wanted to do.

She yawned and settled back on her heels.

Hunter continued to run his hand over her, along her throat, then downward. He trailed his fingers over the swell of her breast. She became very still. Her nipple beaded. She hoped he wouldn't notice. He moved his hand to her shoulder.

She yawned again. The sofa was roomy enough for two. Would he mind if she lay next to him?

"Lie down," he said, reading her thoughts.

She slid onto the sofa, turning her back to him when he rolled onto his side and made room for her. She snagged the afghan and pulled it up. He covered them. She closed her eyes wearily. Her face ached, but she was otherwise warm and comfortable. Lying there was nice.

Hunter seemed to be sound asleep. She wasn't at all sleepy. The blood hummed through her veins in a steady rhythm. Her heartbeat increased as awareness of his solid strength stole over her.

When his arm slid over her, she held her breath, then relaxed. He rubbed lightly over her abdomen, then paused and gingerly explored the lump that indicated the presence of their child. His touch was gentle and soothing.

This was really nice. She could get used to it. To him. To living here…

She drifted into a world of soft colors and strokes and whispers of something or other. She couldn't quite catch the words.

Celia opened her eyes. She was still lying in Hunter's arms, locked against his warmth. The sky had darkened to deep twilight, but the shadows in the great room were friendly. The chill of night hadn't penetrated the house yet. Or maybe she didn't feel it because of the heat thrown off by Hunter's body.

Carefully, she stretched her legs, then eased onto her back so she could look at her sleeping husband.

He had a strong angular face, but his mouth saved it from severity. The suggestion of a cleft in his chin made him irresistible. She had always longed to kiss him there.

She did so now, having to move her head only slightly to reach him.

His eyes opened.

She held her breath and prayed he would go back to sleep, losing her foolish action to dreams he wouldn't recall when he awoke. No such luck.

He blinked his beautiful eyes, then continued to stare at her until she trembled from the effort of not moving. He lifted his hand and touched her cheek.

The swelling had gone down quite a bit. She could move her mouth without grimacing.

He curled one finger under her chin, positioning her head so he could study the injury. Softly, so softly, he began to stroke her bottom lip with his thumb. She held as still as a rabbit while her heart started to pound in heavy, earthshaking beats.

His gaze continued to hold hers.

She desperately wanted him to kiss her, to take her to that magic place they'd visited at New Year's, to make her his wife in all the ways—

Her breath caught. He was... He was going to...

Lips as gentle as the fluttering fall of a rose petal touched her mouth. He kissed along her jaw, careful of her cheek, then back to her lips. His mouth settled over hers.

The kiss stayed that way—the gentlest of exploring touches—for a long time while he moved from one side of her face to the other.

Wave after wave of electricity arced between them each time his mouth swept over hers. It spread in ripples throughout her body. She was drowning, dying, going down in flames, going up in smoke....

Unable to stay still, she moved her lips ever so slightly and spread her fingers over his flesh. His chest hair prickled her palms as she flattened them against him.

His tongue parted her lips as if her movements were the invitation he'd been waiting for. He outlined her lips, then explored the edge of her teeth. When he stroked her tongue, she couldn't hold back any longer.

She answered every move of his with a like one of her own. Finally, she dared to slide her right arm around him and run her hand over his back.

He took the kiss deeper, harder.

A restless need engulfed her. She moved against

him, sliding her leg over his hip so she could get closer. A tremor rolled over her as she felt the hard strength of his erection against the apex of her legs.

Passion burned past any caution she might have felt at their mindless actions. This was Hunter, the man she'd chosen to father her child, the man she'd married.

She arched against him, her moan of need telling him how much she wanted his solid warmth inside her.

His hands caressed her back, then slid under her shirt. His fingers were slightly rough from calluses, but his touch was exquisite.

"I loved your gentleness," she murmured, recalling the bliss she'd found with this man and only this man. "You were so gentle and yet so grand."

"Was I?"

The question was idle, almost amused, except for the serious intensity that blazed in his eyes as he lifted himself to his elbow and gazed down at her.

"Oh, yes. You were wonderful."

He shifted them, tucking her farther under his body and sliding one hard thigh between her legs. She moved so that their hips rubbed, fabric on fabric, a whisper of sound, a soft, tearing sigh of impatience.

She wanted their clothing gone.

With his right hand tangled in her hair, he used his left one on her shirt, quickly unfastening it and pushing it to the side. In an easy demonstration of his dexterity, he reached behind her and unsnapped her bra. Soon both it and the shirt landed on the floor.

He cupped her breast in his hand, hefting its weight

and fit in his palm. "Did I touch you here that night?"

"Yes."

She closed her eyes as ecstasy wrapped around her in tight circles of delight. She stroked his smooth skin, ran her fingertips through the crinkly hairs on his chest and explored the nipple until it formed a tight ball the way hers did under his touch.

He shifted again, sliding downward until he could take her burgeoning breast in his mouth. Gasps of pleasure were torn from her as he teased her with his tongue and teeth and lips until she writhed against him.

At last, he skimmed a hand downward, pausing when he encountered her jeans. He quickly unfastened them and slipped inside. Cupping his palm over her, he explored and caressed until wild passion bloomed in her.

She moaned his name as moisture slicked and readied her for his final caress. His mouth came back to hers. They plunged into the kiss while desire soared between them.

Her hands shaking, she found the snap and zipper on his jeans and pushed the material out of the way. Sliding her fingers under the waistband of his briefs, she returned his intimate caresses, cupping him in one hand, stroking with the other, until the mindless need could no longer be controlled.

"Wait," he muttered hoarsely.

Pushing her away, he heaved himself up on his arms.

"Now," he said.

She pushed his clothing over his hips and past his

knees. He swung back to his side and kicked them off. Then he stripped her.

The blood raged through her like a sea gone wild, lashing in great swells, driven by the storm of passion that racked them both. When he moved, she opened her legs, ready for him, wanting him at the very center of the tempest.

He settled between her thighs, touching intimately in every part, but not completely. He gave her a whole-body caress, shifting slightly from side to side so that every inch of her knew every inch of him.

Looking into his eyes, she saw knowledge there— a man's awareness of a woman, knowing she was ready for him, that she wanted him and would take him at that moment.

She caught her breath as he lifted away from her.

At that same moment, she felt a contraction inside, the familiar rippling movement that told her the babe growing in her was alive and well. "Our child is restless," she said, smiling up at him.

She knew at once the reminder was wrong.

Hunter froze. He stared at her, all the light in the shadowy room gathering in his eyes as his expression grew bleak and the passion drained from him.

She remembered that April had been pregnant when the accident happened. Swallowing the protest as well as the pity that rose in her, she dropped her hands to her sides when he pushed upward and swung away from her. She crossed her arms over her breasts while he stood and pulled on his pants.

Silent, he gathered the rest of his clothing and paused before leaving the room. He shook his head slightly, as if there were no words to express his feelings.

But she had seen the sorrow in his eyes and didn't need words to tell her that he was missing something she couldn't give him—the return of all he'd lost.

Chapter Nine

Celia opened the door and inhaled the rich aroma of the mountain air. Spring had arrived at last. March had been cold and snowy. April had been cold and rainy. May was gorgeous—warm days and crisp nights, sunshine and cloudless skies, wildflowers on every hill and in every meadow.

Since the late-winter snows hadn't been deep enough to halt school and thus use up the scheduled snow days, classes had let out on the thirtieth. That was yesterday.

She laid a hand over her tummy, which looked as if she'd swallowed a large cantaloupe, and experienced a surge of pride as she felt the quickening of life within her.

J.J. entered the kitchen. Stopping beside her, he rested his head on the curve of her hip.

She gave him her very brightest smile. "Hi, sleepy-head. I thought I was going to have to drag you out of bed. We're supposed to plant our geraniums today, remember?"

He smiled and nodded.

"Here, feel," she invited. She laid his hand on the spot where the growing child stretched and kicked. At his round-eyed look, she laughed. "It's your sister. Feels as if she might be a kick boxer or karate expert, huh?"

The five-month sonogram had disclosed the gender of the babe she carried. Her heart jumped into her throat each time she thought of having this tiny girl-child to love. With the joy came the pulse of sadness that she couldn't share her happiness with the child's father.

J.J. laid both hands over the spot and pressed. The baby kicked harder. J.J. giggled.

"Hey, I think she likes you." Celia placed a bowl on the table and filled it with cereal. She put his milk in a cup and snapped the sipping lid on. "Your mommy let me feel you kick once when I spent Christmas with my grandparents. I was surprised at how strong you were."

"Hmm," he said.

"Here're some new postcards from your Grandma McLean."

She let him look at them while he was eating. She went back to work. She was preparing an early lunch for the men. They would be moving cattle for the rest of the day.

She winced slightly as the baby turned somersaults. "Hey, down there," she said to her child, "this is *your* mommy talking. Don't be so rambunctious, you hear?''

J.J. grinned while she fussed, then went back to picking out his favorite pieces of cereal and popping them into his mouth. When he finished, he brought out the photo album she'd found in the study while dusting.

After rinsing her hands, she poured a glass of milk and sat at the table beside her stepson. She kissed the top of his head, then opened the album that they had looked at several times each day since she'd come upon it. He never tired of going through it. In it, he was discovering a sense of himself as a desired and much-loved child.

She hoped.

"The life and times of John Jackson McLean," she read. "That's you. J.J. stands for John Jackson. Here's a picture when you were an hour old. The nurse put a cap on your head to keep you warm. Isn't that cute?" She gave him a hug and held him close. "I hope our new baby will be as smart as you are. As her big brother, you'll have to teach her lots of things."

J.J. gave her a questioning look.

"How to fish and track a bear. How to ride. I saw you on a horse by yourself the other day. Weren't you scared?"

He shook his head.

"Well, you and your daddy are really brave—that's what I think. Oh, look, here's a lock of your baby hair. It's white-blond like your mommy's hair." She ran a hand through his dark strands. "Now it's dark like your daddy's."

He touched her hair, which was pulled up into a ponytail.

"Mine has blond streaks because I comb peroxide through it a couple of times a month. Don't tell anyone. It's a secret." She put a finger over her lips.

His laughter, no longer with a hand over his mouth, warmed her heart. She talked to him constantly and asked his opinion often. Sometimes he hummed with her when she sang a song. Two days ago, he'd opened his mouth and acted as if he were going to sing the words, but he hadn't.

"The teachers gave me a baby shower before school was out. Now we have a baby book to fill in when our new baby gets here this fall. Don't let me forget the lock of hair. Of course, she may be bald when she's born. I looked just like that picture of your Grandpa Ericson—bald on top with a fringe of hair over my ears, when I was born."

They were both laughing when a noise outside drew their attention to the open door. "Let's go see what's happening," she suggested.

She and J.J. walked out on the patio. J.J. took her hand and urged her down to the paddock where Hunter and Jackson were attempting to unload a horse from a trailer.

A rancher from a nearby spread climbed out of the pickup and cursed as the horse kicked the back of the trailer. He stopped when Hunter pointed toward them.

He was invariably polite around her nowadays—more so than when they were first married. He kept his feelings, whatever they were, completely hidden. Since that evening of kisses on the sofa he'd been careful not to touch her.

"Stand back," he ordered now, as if afraid she might leap right into the middle of the action.

"Okay," she said.

"Let's back the trailer into the paddock and leave the stud there until he gets used to things," Jackson said in his understated way.

"Right," Hunter agreed.

The rancher climbed into the pickup and backed through the open gate. They disconnected the trailer and closed the gate. Jackson opened the back of the trailer and did a graceful jump onto the top rail and over the fence.

The stallion suddenly burst from the enclosed space and raced around the paddock, snorting with rage. Rearing up, he lashed out at the trailer and struck it several ringing blows with his iron-clad front hooves.

Celia shrank from the fence and the furious animal confined within. The three men leaned their elbows on the top railing and observed the stallion.

"Think you can do anything with him?" the rancher asked, glancing at the two brothers.

Hunter shrugged. "Maybe. We'll give it a go."

"Well, you don't have to pay anything if you can't get him gentled down. I feel like shooting him. Damned brute killed my best mare. Broke her neck."

Celia gasped. She knew that bears sometimes killed a sow who was protecting her young from him, but she didn't know other animals did.

"I'll put him down if he harms anything on the ranch," Jackson stated.

She didn't know him well, but there was quiet certitude in the way Jackson spoke that told her he wasn't joking. Hunter didn't contradict the statement.

When the stallion raced to the other end of the field, the men removed the trailer. The rancher hooked up and left them with a tip of his hat.

Celia edged nearer the fence. Jackson told them he'd see them later and rode off on a cow pony he was training. She and J.J. stood close to Hunter and watched the stallion run like a whirlwind from one end of the field to the other.

"Are you buying him?" she asked.

"Yes." He barely glanced at her.

"Why?"

"He has the finest bloodlines in the state."

She studied the long-limbed horse. "Other than bears, I didn't know animals killed their females."

"They don't, usually."

"Why did he kill the mare?"

Hunter shifted his gaze from the horse to her. "He was too rough. He'll have to be taught how to be gentle."

"You're going to mate the ranch stock to him?"

"Yes."

She pressed her hands to her heart. "Are you going to tie them up?"

"Their hind legs."

"So they can't kick him?"

"That's right."

Lab came bounding up. After licking her hand, he dashed to J.J. and demanded to be petted. The boy and the dog ran across the road to the yard, now green with spring grass. J.J. found a short stick to throw. Lab barked, joyous with the game.

Celia stared over the railing at the stallion, which had returned to their end of the paddock. He looked

proud and fierce and beautiful in a wild, awesome
way. So did Jackson's black stallion, but without being mean into the bargain.

She clutched Hunter's arm as the studhorse trumpeted into the air, challenging any who would thwart
him. "I don't think you should have brought that
monster here. He's vicious. What if he gets loose?"

"He won't," Hunter said, still in that polite manner
he used with her. "If it makes you feel any better,
he'll be muzzled, too, so he can't bite."

He withdrew his arm, then walked off. A few
minutes later, he came out of the stable riding a roan
gelding. He called to J.J., lifted the boy into the saddle
in front of him and urged the gelding into a brisk trot.
The black Lab bounded along at their heels.

Behind Celia, the stallion snorted.

She moved away from the fence just as the horse
stuck his head over, his teeth bared, ready to bite
anything close. She stared into his angry eyes while
premonitions of danger warned her to flee. She stood
her ground for a second, then hurried to the safety of
the house and the solace she found in the smoothly
running routine she'd established there.

The cowboys took their plates out onto the patio.
Dawn helped Celia carry out tall glasses of iced tea
to them. Hunter and Jackson and J.J. were already at
the limed-oak table in the kitchen. They discussed the
new stud, which had been in residence for a week.

"If the fighting streak goes through the blood-
lines," Jackson was saying when the women returned
and joined them, "we can sell them for rodeo po-
nies."

"If you can breed the mares to him," Dawn warned. "I think it's more than a fighting streak. The stallion could be insane. That can happen to animals as well as humans."

Celia envied Dawn's easy knowledge and experience. Unable to contribute to the conversation, she kept her mouth shut and listened. The more she heard about the stallion, the more uneasy she became.

"Everything is delicious," Dawn remarked during a lull in the conversation. "I've heard about your cooking from the cowboys. I think Jackson is envious. His culinary skills and mine run along the same lines."

"Yeah," he agreed, his attractive half-smile lighting his face. "Wielding a can opener is tough." He smiled at Celia. "This is the best trout I've ever eaten, even better than my Aunt Maggie's."

"Thank you," Celia replied, casting an oblique glance at Hunter to see how he took the compliments.

"What's your secret?" Dawn wanted to know.

"I sprinkled the fish with pepper, garlic and Parmesan cheese, then I dipped it in beer batter. I sauté rather than fry. It takes less oil that way."

Hunter said nothing during this exchange, but she was pleased when both men took second helpings. At least he liked one thing that she did, she mused, taking comfort in small accomplishments.

Dawn drank from her iced tea and set the glass down. "How are you feeling?"

"Fine."

"Are you over the queasiness? Hunter said you were having problems all day."

"Not anymore. It seems to have passed."

"That's great." Dawn gave her an encouraging smile.

Celia wondered when Hunter had discussed her condition with his sister-in-law. She found she didn't like the idea of him talking about it with anyone else—not even someone as kind as Dawn. He should talk to *her*....

She heaved an internal sigh. She and Hunter usually talked about schedules or picking up medicine at the vet's office. He never spoke to her about her health or well-being. He never mentioned the coming child at all.

At times she'd wanted to scream at him about that or burst into tears, but she hadn't. The emotional loops had calmed down a lot as her pregnancy progressed and the hormones weren't quite so crazy.

She wanted Hunter to be as excited about their child as she was. Realistically, she knew that wasn't going to happen.

When despair threatened, as it sometimes did, or when she wanted to beg for some sign of feeling from him or simply ask him to talk to her, she refrained. After the child came, then she would make a decision concerning the marriage and whether it should be continued. She would have to put the baby's welfare first.

A shimmer of pain pinged like an echo of loneliness through her as she thought of the future.

"The fish bothered you earlier," Hunter said suddenly.

The three adults and J.J. looked at him.

"Oh, that's right. It did. When I first opened the

bag, the scent got to me for a minute.'' She smiled brightly to show she was fine now.

It surprised her that Hunter had noticed her reaction. He'd come into the house when she'd started the meal. He'd been working with the cattle all week, putting tags in their ears, checking them for pinkeye and parasites, counting them and their young, then moving them to pastures farther up in the mountains as the weather warmed.

"How's it going with the training?" he asked Jackson.

Jackson chuckled. "The stallion has more mean ideas than a snake in a henhouse."

"Did you get a saddle on him?"

"Yes. I worked him on a lunge for a while, then rode him in the paddock for an hour. He did okay, but I wouldn't trust him out on a trail."

"He tried to bite the mare when she got too close to the fence. I moved her to the pasture on the other side of our place," Dawn said. She shook her head. "I don't like him. He's got killer instincts."

Celia gasped, then stared at Hunter. "And you plan to keep him?" She gestured toward J.J. "With children here?"

"Jackson and I can handle him. Stay away from the paddock," he warned. He gave J.J. a stern look. "You, too. You understand?"

J.J. nodded at once.

Celia saw Jackson and Dawn exchange glances and knew they wondered at the hard tone. She downright resented it, for both the boy's sake and her own. Since it was a safety issue and she didn't trust her emotions at present, she maintained a smiling silence.

When the main course was over, she and Dawn served pie and coffee to the men out on the patio. The cowboys ambled off to the bunkhouse after that. Dawn sat beside Jackson on the swing. J.J. played in the yard with Lab.

Celia watched the color of the sunset fade into the rosy magenta of twilight. She was aware of Hunter seated beside her. His long legs enabled his feet to touch the ground while hers dangled a few inches short. She hooked her ankles together and swung back and forth.

Catching a movement from the corner of her eye, she glanced over in time to see Jackson lay his hand on Dawn, his fingers splayed out over the light blue of her slacks as he lightly caressed her abdomen.

A chill raced up her spine at the look in his eyes. Fierce. Possessive. Tender. Intense. Loving.

All those and more.

Dawn placed her lovely, long-fingered hand over his, her skin a pale feminine contrast to his masculine darkness, her white-blond hair close to his black locks. She looked at her husband and smiled. They looked like a couple deeply in love.

Celia swallowed as unexpected yearning formed a solid ache inside her. An intuition bloomed in her consciousness.

"You're pregnant," she said, blurting it out without thinking.

Dawn started in surprise, then laughed with pure happiness. "Yes, I am. At least we think so, but it's early, yet. I've only used a test from the drugstore."

Jackson moved his hand, but his arm lazily encircled his wife's shoulders. He and Hunter exchanged glances, then watched the sunset again.

"I understand they're pretty reliable," Celia quickly reassured the other woman. "If it says you're expecting, you most likely are."

"I hope so. We've been trying for months." Dawn stopped when she realized what she had said, then covered her mouth and burst into laughter.

Jackson gave an amused snort. "It was tough work, but somebody had to do it."

They all laughed.

Celia's gaze collided with Hunter's. She felt herself grow warm. It had only taken them one time—well, actually two, but they'd both been on the same night—for him to get her in the family way.

Maybe that was an omen. Maybe their child and marriage were meant to be. And maybe she was grasping at straws to justify her foolish, impulsive action that night.

"It's time for J.J. to get ready for bed," Hunter said, standing and calling for his son.

J.J. and Lab dashed over to them. The boy leaned against her knees. The dog licked her hand until she patted his head and scratched his ears. He pressed against her knees, too. She hugged J.J. and stood.

"Shall I run your bathwater?" she asked.

J.J. nodded, gave Lab a squeeze around the neck and then hugged Dawn and Jackson. He hesitated in front of his father. Hunter scooped him into his arms. "I'll handle his bath. You can take it easy."

J.J. looked downward, then pointed to Celia, making it clear that he preferred her.

Celia saw the flash of stark pain in Hunter's eyes

before he smiled and set J.J. down. "Looks as if you've been pegged for duty," he said easily. "I'll clean up the kitchen instead. That's a fair deal, huh?"

"Oh, yes," she said.

"I'll help," Dawn volunteered.

Hunter shook his head. "We can handle it. You two go plan your nursery."

Celia smiled the whole time they said good-night, then she slipped inside, leaving Hunter and his son to come in when they were done. She ran the water in the tub and waited for J.J. to appear. When he did, she let him play in the water until his fingers and toes were shriveled.

"Look at that," she mock-scolded. "You're turning into a prune before my very eyes."

He giggled and flicked his fingers at her, then ducked his head bashfully.

"Oh, the old splash-'em-in-the-face trick, huh? Just for that..." She squirted him with a rubber whale.

Looking up, she saw Hunter leaning against the doorframe, his eyes like twin pits into hell.

For a heartbeat, she felt pity for him, then she looked away. She couldn't help him. He'd cut himself off from his son. As far as she could tell, he hadn't heeded her advice about smiling at all.

She unplugged the tub and rinsed J.J., and the toys she'd let him take into the bath, with the hose attachment. She dried him off and helped him with his pajamas. Hunter picked the child up when it was time to go.

He carried his son to bed and tucked him in, then reached for the switch on the lamp.

J.J. gave Celia a pleading glance.

"We...we read a book before he goes to sleep," she said before Hunter could turn the light off.

J.J. grabbed the baby album and held it defensively against his narrow chest. Celia had an idea.

"I'm pretty tired. Perhaps you could read to him tonight." She backed toward the door. "I'll go on to bed."

Before she could change her mind, she rushed from the room and down the hall. She closed the door to her bedroom and leaned against it, her heart pounding. She closed her eyes and prayed that Hunter would be okay.

The baby book, with its pictures of him and April and J.J., was going to cut deep. She didn't know if she'd done the right thing or not, but she felt she had to reach Hunter before he lost his son completely.

She pressed her ear to the door and waited forever, it seemed, until she heard his footsteps in the hall. He paused outside her door—she wondered if he could hear her heart pounding—before going on to his own room.

Finally, exhaling the tension that had built to unbearable heights during the past half hour, she prepared for bed. Later, wearing the large T-shirt she slept in during the summer months, she reviewed one of her child-psychology books before going to bed.

At ten, she snapped the lamp off and snuggled down under the covers. She watched the stars twinkle through the open window for a long time before she went to sleep.

She woke at midnight.

She lay still for a few minutes, wondering what had disturbed her. Lab wasn't barking, so she was sure no intruder had entered the house. The coyote chorus wasn't giving a performance.

After several minutes, she decided a glass of warm milk would put her back to sleep. She climbed out of the cozy bed and slipped on the fleecy moccasins she wore in the house.

In the kitchen, she poured a cup of skim milk and heated it in the microwave. Sipping from the cup, she leaned against the counter and gazed out at the night.

A tremor shook her when she spied the bulky form of her husband on the patio. He sat on the steps, his hands tucked into his armpits to keep them warm while he stared off into space. She felt his sadness as if it were a tangible thing.

She longed to go to him and offer the comfort of her arms and whatever else he wanted to take from her, but she didn't. His cool rejection was more than she could bear at this moment; she might burst into tears.

She gulped the milk down and hurried back to bed.

Sometime later—she didn't know how long—she heard the quiet opening and closing of the door, then his steps in the hallway. Again she heard his pause outside her door.

The knob turned, and a dark figure entered the room as silently as a ghost. Her heart beat so hard she wondered that he didn't hear it when he stopped beside her bed.

He stood there for several long minutes. At last she could stand it no longer. She opened her eyes to see what he was doing.

In the inky gloom, the shadows seemed more pronounced, but she could see his eyes. He was simply standing there, watching her. An impulse stronger than common sense gripped her. She rose to her knees and took him in her arms.

The nighttime cold clung to his clothing. She held him closer. He shifted. She expected him to pull away, but his hands touched her shoulders. His arms slipped around her. For several minutes, he held her, then he quietly left.

She inhaled carefully, as if she might shatter, when the door closed. She tossed restlessly after that, unable to really sleep. At three, a cry rent the dark.

"Mommy! Mommy!"

Sitting up in bed, she realized J.J. was screaming. A nightmare. She jumped from the bed and raced down the hall. Hunter was a step behind her.

She fumbled with the light pull and finally got it on. "J.J., honey, wake up," she said, reaching for him.

He threw himself at her, wrapping his arms around her neck, his legs around her waist. "Mommy," he said.

She met Hunter's gaze above the boy's head. She couldn't read his expression. He'd closed himself off completely from any emotion.

"There, there," she crooned. "It's okay. I'm here. Your daddy is, too. We'll stay with you."

Hunter reached for J.J., a worried frown indenting two lines between his eyebrows.

J.J. clung to her. "No," he cried. He buried his face against her. "Mommy," he said. "Mommy stay."

She felt his hot, wet tears on her neck. His body shook with sobs. Tears filled her eyes.

Hunter dropped his hands to his sides.

She stood there helplessly, not knowing what to do.

Hunter spun and walked out.

"There, there," she said, patting J.J.'s back. She sat in the rocker and held him.

Out in the graveled area in front of the ranch buildings, she saw headlights come on. Hunter turned the pickup and headed off down the road. She willed him to come back, but he didn't.

Silence spread over the ranch with the settling of the gravel dust in his wake. It shrouded her spirit and drew a sharp sigh from her.

She sat there long after J.J. fell asleep, holding him against her heart while the new life fluttered and stirred within her.

Chapter Ten

Celia watched the men remove hay from the upper section of the cattle barn. Hunter was stacking the bales on the hay wagon. She stretched her swollen feet out on the swing and observed her husband for several minutes before making up her mind to act.

When he'd finished and jumped off the wagon, she slipped on her sandals and pushed herself upright. The breeze caught her maternity top and plastered it to her body. She looped her arms across her waist, self-conscious about her rotund silhouette.

Hunter glanced up. No smile graced his stern face at her approach. Tom shifted so he could see what Hunter was looking at. The older man's welcoming smile made her feel better.

"Good morning," she said to both of them. She looked directly at Hunter. "I'd like to speak to you, please."

"I'll check those calves," Tom said and hurried off.

Celia walked toward the house, not wanting to stray too far. J.J. was in the living room, watching a video. He'd slept late that morning and seemed unaware of the events of the night before. She stopped under the oak tree halfway between the barn and the house.

Looking at Hunter's closed, dark face, she experienced a surge of sympathy so strong she nearly reached for him. But now wasn't the time. She was also angry.

"You were gone all night," she said.

He braced a hand on his outthrust hip and stood there staring into space. He flicked her a glance that told her not to push it.

The sympathy faded while the anger bloomed. If they were to be a family, some things had to be ironed out.

"I don't care where you were. What I do care about is how you treat me, your wife, and how you treat J.J., your son. That concerns me."

A spasm of emotion passed over his face, but he didn't say a word, only nodded as if giving her permission to go on with her tirade.

"I didn't tell J.J. to call me mother. Not once. Not ever. I have told him about April. My God, Hunter, he didn't even know her name! His own mother. I found the album and I showed him pictures of you three as a family. I thought it was important that he feel a part of you and April, that he be reminded that he was loved."

She had to stop as she nearly choked on the word. Hunter watched her, as impassive as a statue.

Tears pressed close to the surface. She'd die rather than cry in front of him. "Everyone needs to feel wanted. Even you, although I doubt if you'll admit it. J.J. needs attention. And…I… I need…"

For him to come to her last night, to share that moment of tenderness, then to leave because a child needed her, had left her too vulnerable. The anger grew.

"I thought we could at least deal kindly with each other, maybe even find happiness, but I was wrong. I'm sick of your surliness. I'm tired of your silence. I didn't ask for this marriage. You were the one who insisted on it. I've done my share. Now…now it's up to you."

He didn't move a hair.

The anger boiled higher. "My life was fine before our marriage. I don't need you in any way, shape or form. I can make it on my own."

"Is that right?" His tone was deadly quiet. "What about your job? Would you have kept it without marriage? I don't think so. Would your friends have rallied around you? I doubt it. Without a job and friends, what would you do?"

She gave him the same stony glare he gave her. "I could make it for a year. I still can." She walked off.

He followed at her heels. "How? You've rented your house. Are you going to demand that they leave?"

She frowned. She couldn't go back on her word. He was right. She had no place to go. "I can live with my mother," she declared, mentally shying from the notion.

He rocked back and crossed his arms. "Yes, there is that possibility. How long has it been since you lived at home, under your mother's thumb, her telling you what you're doing wrong every minute of every day?"

"How can that be any worse than here?" she said, a comment, not really a question. "I wouldn't have to live with your scowls and scoldings and staying out all night, leaving me sleepless and worried...."

Well, enough of that. She wasn't going to admit to waiting for the phone to ring and the sheriff telling her Hunter had wrapped his truck around a telephone pole.

His chest expanded as if he held himself in check with an effort. "You've retained your job and your standing in the community—some would even say it's gone up—because of marriage to me. Don't tell me you haven't gotten anything out of it."

"Ha. I should have stayed in Reno. At least people mind their own business in a city. I can move there—"

"No!" a childish treble cried. J.J. burst from the house and flung himself across the patio into her arms. "Don't," he said. "Don't go."

Celia held the child's trembling body against her. "Don't cry," she whispered. "No one's going to go anywhere. Your daddy and I were having a quarrel. People say things then that they're sorry for later. No one's leaving."

In that moment, she knew she couldn't leave this lonely little boy. His young spirit might not recover if he was abandoned by another person he'd come to trust.

"Shh, I love you," she murmured. "I love you. I won't leave you, not ever. I love you." She swung him from side to side, soothing and whispering to him, pressing kisses on his temple and cheek.

A hand touched her shoulder.

She lifted her head from the child's and stared into Hunter's forest-green eyes. He looked haunted and full of misery. She looked away. Her sympathy was for his son.

Hunter moved his hand from her to J.J. and tousled the child's hair. "No one is leaving," he assured J.J., his tone deeper than usual. He cleared his throat. "Celia can't leave us. The flowers you two planted haven't bloomed yet."

J.J. snuggled his face into Celia's neck. He listened intently as Hunter mentioned other activities on the ranch that he and his son needed to do. Then Lab spotted J.J. and came bounding up with a stick in his mouth.

"Lab," J.J. said, wanting down. "Here, boy." He threw the stick, then he and the dog chased after it.

"He's talked to the dog," Hunter said. "Before this."

"Yes, I've heard him."

"But he wouldn't talk to me."

"Until now."

Hunter sat down heavily on the planking. "He talked to you, not me. He doesn't trust me."

"You'll have to give him time. I think he's opening up, but don't rush him or try to force him to speak."

Hunter heaved a deep breath and gazed up at her.

She shifted nervously from one foot to the other. She was aware of the swelling and the ache in her ankles.

"I drove up to the fire lookout last night," he said. "I slept in the truck. One of the forest rangers woke me when he came to check the tower this morning. I had coffee with him and came home."

She nodded and shifted her weight again.

"Are you hurting?" he asked.

Surprised, she nodded. "My feet ache. I'm having trouble with them swelling."

"Go sit in the swing," he suggested. "I'll fix lunch." He placed a chair so she could prop her feet up after she was seated. "I apologize for...not being kind," he said after an awkward moment. "You have to stay. J.J. needs you."

She nodded. "I'll tell him to call me Celia."

"No. Let him call you whatever feels right."

He returned her gaze when she stared at him, wary of this kinder, gentler stranger.

"You don't trust me," he said. "I can't say I blame you. I've been unfair, resentful of the marriage I insisted on. I'll try to be a better husband."

With that, he walked into the house. With one foot, she pushed the swing into motion while she watched her stepson and his dog play in the yard.

Inside, she could hear Hunter busy at his task. Tom drove down the road, a tractor attached to the hay wagon. Jackson worked with a young horse in a paddock. Dawn and her mother walked through a field of herbs, inspecting the plants and chatting. Their three workers picked leaves and laid them on screens to dry in the sun. Along the slope of a far hill, the cowhands moved a small herd to summer pasture.

It was a beautiful scene, right out of a book. However, try as she would, she couldn't believe it was quite real.

"Hunter?"

He glanced over his shoulder. Celia wore a worried frown. She was dressed in pink-and-white checked shorts and a T-shirt with sleeves that matched them. Her hair was tucked on top of her head in deference to the July heat.

Now in her seventh month, she was amusingly rotund, but he found his pulse speeding up as he glanced past her waist to her legs. She'd acquired a light tan while working with the flowers she and J.J. had planted, and she looked healthy and sexy as hell.

"Yeah?" he said, straightening from the tractor he was working on.

"Uh, I... My father and I E-mail each other fairly often."

He nodded. He knew she'd installed her computer and several other items from her house in her bedroom. She was finishing a six-week course through a university summer-school program. Her final exam—an essay on early-childhood learning disorders—was due next week. He'd heard her pecking away at the homework many nights after J.J. had gone to bed. He'd also learned she sent it in via the Internet.

"My dad and stepmother—uh, your aunt—would like to stop by for a night or two next week. Would that be okay?"

Kerri was blood kin. Hugh was his father-in-law. He could hardly refuse. "Of course."

Her smile was instantaneous. "Great."

He went back to work. He was aware when she crept closer. The scent of her perfume overrode the smell of oil and diesel fumes from the tractor. He inhaled, taking the enticing aroma of her deep inside him.

The image this produced shook him, and he nearly dropped the hose clamp. He attached the new hose, then rubbed a grease remover into his hands and wiped them on a rag. His gaze was drawn like a magnet to those shapely legs, then upward to her anxious smile.

His sleep had been restless of late. He'd made a vow to be a better father and husband. To that end, he'd tried to include them in his life. He invited them to accompany him on his trips to town, often taking them to the restaurant by the lake to eat since he'd discovered it was her favorite place.

Following Celia's example, he made a point of laughing and joking with J.J. while they took turns throwing a stick or ball for the Lab. At dinner each night, he told stories about the ranch, recounting funny incidents but also keeping Celia posted about the work that was needed to keep it going. She was an inspiring listener, interested and seemingly impressed with everything he did. He'd found himself talking a lot more about his plans and ideas the past three weeks than he had the previous three years.

He'd told her of his growing respect for his half brother and that Jackson was easy to work with, once he'd gotten to know him.

"And after you both quit wearing those cumbersome chips on your shoulders?" she had teased, understanding exactly how those first few months had gone.

And they'd laughed together. So had J.J.

"Uh, there's one more thing," she said now.

He was used to her dithering ways. He wondered what it was about her past life that had made her always hesitant to bring up a new subject, as if she thought it might offend the other person. He didn't like the picture this suggested.

Watching her with his son, he'd decided she was a warm and caring person. It was obvious J.J. adored her. It only took the tiniest frown from her for the boy to straighten up if he wasn't acting right.

She always explained why things were the way they were when she had to reprimand him. Then she would kiss him, assure him she loved him and send him about his business.

A natural mother.

A strange sensation churned inside him, as if a giant fist had invaded and was twisting his insides into knots.

"Speak," he invited, smiling now to assure her that, whatever she had on her mind, it was okay.

"I'd like to have J.J.'s birthday party while my folks are here. I thought we could grill hamburgers. He asked for them the other night. And I'd like to give him a pony of his own as a birthday present. If you don't mind."

The last request took him by surprise. It must have shown on his face. She cast him an almost-pleading glance. It made him wonder about himself that his wife and child were both wary of him at times.

"A pony, huh? That's a good idea."

She smiled eagerly, looking like a young girl, happy and beautiful and full of life.

He gazed at her very plump middle. His heart acted oddly—sort of jumping around in his chest as if it were excited. His wife *was* full of life—with his child. Their child. A daughter.

She'd asked him the other day what he thought of the name Margaret Julia, after both their mothers. And did he think his mother would mind? He'd told her his mother would be home in August and she could ask her, but he thought she would be thrilled. Grandmothers were like that.

"You don't have to buy the pony," he continued. "I'll pay for it."

The light in her eyes died.

He realized he'd hurt her feelings. He frowned, not liking that image of himself. "Or we could buy it together and present it from both of us."

"Oh," she said, brightening instantly. "That would be good. He'd like that. It would be like a real family."

Like a real family.

The words drummed in his brain. There was the key to their future. He knew it, felt it all the way to his bones. But the question was, could he ever be a real husband to this woman he'd so precipitously married?

Celia woke with a shriek. She sat up in bed, her heart pounding in fright. Her eyes were open, but she couldn't see a thing in the stygian darkness.

Another lightning bolt cut across the sky; the thunder from the first one rolled over the house and echoed from the hills. The clap from the second bolt cracked and rumbled before the first had died away.

Drawing her knees up as far as she could, Celia wrapped her arms around them and watched nature's awesome display across the night sky.

She'd seen the heat lightning of summer hit a tree and cause it to explode into a million flying fragments. She'd seen forest fires started that way. Her beloved grandfather had died fighting one of those fires.

As a retired forest ranger, he had often volunteered his services when the fires got bad. Although he hadn't been at the front lines of the fire, he'd been trapped in a tent where they'd set up headquarters when the fire had crowned and encircled the camp.

She'd been eighteen at the time and had spent the rest of the summer with her grandmother, the two of them joined in grief and love. Lightning always gave her an anxious feeling, as if the fates were angry...

A movement at the corner of her eye caused her to gasp.

Hunter entered her room. "I thought I heard something."

"It was nothing— I mean, it was me, but it's okay. The storm woke me. For a minute, I thought the lightning had hit the house or something."

He sat on the bed.

She felt his heat instantly. It was comforting. She resisted an urge to lean into him. Her breath hitched when he moved closer. His arm dropped around her shoulders.

"You're trembling," he murmured.

His breath fanned against her neck as he spoke. To

her shock and consternation, he kissed her temple, then lingered to rub his chin against her hair.

"I... Storms scare me. Sometimes. Actually, it's the lightning. My granddad..." She trailed off. He didn't want to know about her past.

"I remember him," Hunter said in a reminiscent tone. "He gave a lecture to our class once on safety in the woods, especially during a fire."

"He was killed in a fire."

"I know. It was a loss to the community."

She sighed and leaned against his solid warmth, comforted by his words. "My father's parents died before I could really know them, but I stayed with my mother's folks a lot when I was growing up. Mom took classes so she could become a paralegal. After the divorce, she started her own title-search company and was even busier."

"I knew all my grandparents. The men died of heart attacks in their fifties, but the women lived into their seventies. Dad was nearly forty when he and Mom married, she was over thirty, so all my relatives seemed old to me."

"I don't think J.J. will remember either grandfather when he grows up, but it's nice that he has his grandmothers so close. Family is an important legacy to a child."

He stroked through her hair, then slipped his hand under the fall and laid it on her neck. She was so aware of him, her skin felt as if every nerve was attuned to his presence and the slightest movement he made.

They watched the lightning until the clouds rolled on over the mountain and disappeared. A sliver of a moon hung over the landscape. The wind, chilly after the storm, stirred the curtains at her window.

"Do you keep the window open at night?" he asked.

She nodded, then cleared her throat. "Yes."

He moved, causing her to tense. She prepared for his departure. Instead, his free hand touched her arm, slid past it and came to rest on her tummy.

Gently, he explored the tight basketball-like roundness. She was terribly self-conscious about her figure now, feeling awkward and unattractive. Her feet swelled in the afternoons, and she moved gracelessly through the days.

"April thought she was ugly during her pregnancy," he said. "She wasn't. A woman can be beautiful then, too."

"Oh," she said, as if he'd made a profound statement.

She felt rather than saw his smile. "You're very pretty, did you know that?"

She shook her head.

His hand rubbed back and forth on her belly. The back of it brushed one of her breasts, which were large and heavy. A throbbing sensation pulsed through them. Her nipples contracted into almost-painful knots.

She wondered if he realized what he was doing. His hand brushed her breast with each stroke now. She bit her lip to keep from crying out in frustration. She wanted him to make love to her, but she couldn't ask. She remembered the last time he'd touched her. He'd been moody and distant for a month afterward.

Her breath rasped in her ears. With a startled jerk,

she realized it wasn't just hers. His was loud, too, as he continued to hold and caress her, his head against hers.

She was going to explode if he didn't stop. Her breasts ached with a fullness that bothered her. Her whole body had responded to his light, continual touches with an intensity she couldn't deny.

"I...I think we'd better go to sleep. I mean, to bed, to your bed..." This wasn't coming out at all how she meant it.

"Me, too."

His voice was so husky, it sent shivers down her neck. She felt his lips touch her temple, then her shoulder as he nuzzled aside the loose collar of the T-shirt.

Standing, he swung her up into his arms as easily as if she weighed next to nothing. She threw an arm around his neck in alarm. When he laid her on his bed, she became aware of the arousal behind his unfastened jeans.

He kicked the pants aside and slid under the sheet, pulling it over both of them. She saw the shadow of his face against the darker shadow of the ceiling as he bent over her.

Shocked, she parted her lips, not sure whether she was going to protest or sigh. She did neither.

His lips closed over hers. His tongue invaded her mouth, causing a storm to erupt in her blood. Wildfire roared within her, sending up caution and any sanity she might have mustered in a puff of mindless desire.

She moaned. He answered with a throaty sound, a growl of need that matched the yearning in her. The nameless fears that had gripped her at his first touch relaxed as he continued to stroke gently over her rounded middle.

Finally, his hand drifted upward. He cupped her breast. She drew a deep breath, pushing into his palm as she did so. She moved her leg restlessly and encountered the hard, probing staff of his arousal.

She hesitated, then touched him intimately. He gasped, then moved in her hand. His thigh slipped between hers as he adjusted his body to her shape. Leaning on an elbow, he caressed her with his tongue and his ever-moving hand, building layer upon layer of excitement in her.

Needs long denied shimmered in her, causing her to tremble and thrash gently against him, wanting to be closer and closer until they merged completely.

When he released her mouth, he moved downward, his lips and teeth and tongue tasting, testing, probing her flesh as he explored her breasts, then her belly button.

She closed her eyes and stroked through the dark, silky strands of his hair, letting herself go, forgetting that there was a tomorrow and she would have to face it.

There was only this night, this moment, this terrible, awesome passion…

He shifted again, then nuzzled his face into the springy crest at the apex of her thighs. This was something he'd done before, on New Year's Eve. She'd been surprised, faintly shocked at her body's response, then carried away by wave after wave of reckless desire.

She moaned and panted under the onslaught of his generous lovemaking, completely lost to sensation while he stroked the flames ever higher. When she could stand it no longer, she tugged at his shoulders.

"Come to me. Now. Come to me," she begged, needing him as she'd never needed another.

He rose to his knees and thrust gently into her.

She sighed with relief. She'd been afraid, after that other time, that they wouldn't make it.

Then, suddenly, her fears revived; his desire faded away.

He swung away from her and sat on the side of the bed, his elbows on his knees, his face in his hands. His broad shoulders slumped as he exhaled a heavy sigh.

"It's okay," she said, not sure what to do.

"Is it?" he questioned in a harsh, sarcastic voice. "Is it?" he repeated. He pulled on his clothes and rammed his feet into jogging shoes. "Don't wait up," he advised.

Then he walked out.

She listened for the door to open, for the truck to start up, but neither happened. She tiptoed down the hall.

"Go back to bed," he told her in a low growl.

She slipped down the hall as silently as a wraith. At the door to her room, she paused. Then she turned and went back to his bed. There, she curled up under the sheet and waited. He didn't return to her all night.

At dawn, she dressed and put on a pot of coffee. She found her husband asleep on the sofa, the afghan over him, his bare feet hanging over the end.

She didn't know exactly what was wrong, but she thought only Hunter could overcome it. Maybe he felt guilt at making love to a woman who wasn't his beloved first wife. Maybe he just didn't want her.

An ache settled inside her along with the baby she loved. Confusion whirled through her, messing up her thinking processes. There were only a couple of thoughts clear in her mind.

She felt terribly sad for this strong, handsome, but grieving man she'd married. And she was terribly in love with him.

Chapter Eleven

Celia shifted her weight from one hip to the other. Her feet were propped on the swing. She couldn't remember when she'd last been so miserable. No position was comfortable. Everything about her ached.

"Have you heard from Margaret lately?" Kerri, Hunter's aunt and her stepmother, asked.

Kerri, Dawn and Dawn's mom were seated in lawn chairs so Celia had the patio swing to herself.

"I got a letter yesterday," Hazel Ericson replied. "She's in Greece and having a wonderful time. She said parts of the country remind her of home."

"Traveling was something she always wanted to do," Dawn said. "I can't imagine being away from here for six weeks, much less six months."

Celia pushed the swing into motion and gazed around the patio and yard. Today was J.J.'s birthday, and they were having a cookout at his request.

The pony she and Hunter had bought for him was safely tucked into a stall in the barn on the Ericson place. Dawn and Jackson had secretly been working with the animal for a week, making sure it was perfectly behaved before the birthday bash. Dawn had assured her it was.

Hunter stood in front of the grill, spatula in hand to turn the hamburgers when they were ready. Celia had talked to him about having some of J.J.'s school friends over, but they had decided to limit the informal get-together to the immediate family.

J.J., still shy about talking in front of strangers, had responded immediately to her father. Her dad had been openly delighted with his grandson and had won J.J. over in a twinkling with his praise of Lab and the tricks she and J.J. had taught the dog that summer.

"Watch this, Grandpa!" J.J. called, running back with the stick he'd nabbed from the dog. "Say your prayers," he now ordered his pet.

Lab dropped to the ground, crossed his front feet and laid his chin on them. The effect was only slightly spoiled by the rapid wagging of his tail.

Celia's father laughed heartily and applauded. Lab jumped up and licked the older man on the chin. J.J. leaned against his granddad. He hesitated, then snaked his arm around the man's shoulders in an attitude of trust.

Celia's throat closed up. The boy had been affectionate with Kerri, too. Children instinctively trusted those who were their parents or grandparents.

Glancing at her stepmother, she saw something like sorrow on the older woman's face. Kerri had never been able to have children. As a teenager, Celia had been relieved, but now she sympathized with the other woman.

"I hope you and Dad will be able to visit with us often in the future," she said on impulse.

Kerri, seated in a wicker rocker Celia had rescued from the rafters of the shed, actually looked pleased by the invitation. "I'm sure we will. Hugh loves children."

The words brought back a host of memories for Celia. Her father had attended all her school functions. She'd thought he would always be there for her.

Then he'd left.

Her eyes were drawn to Hunter. She wondered how they could make it without love and caring between them. He must have sensed her scrutiny. His gaze met hers.

Longing, raw and deep, gripped her suddenly. She looked away, afraid he would see the need, embarrassed by the hunger that demanded kisses and ardent caresses.

Yeah, right. As if he would want to make love to someone who looked as if she'd swallowed a watermelon.

She lowered her eyes and stared at her puffy ankles. The sight only reinforced how very unattractive she was at the moment. Inexplicably sad, she wondered what snags in the fabric of time she'd set in motion by her impulsive act on New Year's Eve. She couldn't have wreaked more havoc if she'd *resolved* to cause Hunter as much trouble as she could.

J.J. skipped across the lawn, her father and the Lab behind him. "Is dinner ready?" he asked, rising on tiptoe to peer at the grill.

Hunter lifted him and let him check the burgers. When he set the boy down, J.J. came to her.

"Come on, Grandpa. Sit here with us," he invited.

Celia moved her feet so he could snuggle next to her. He laid his head on her tummy. Her father joined them on the swing. Lab settled against the side of the house, his tongue lolling as he panted to cool off in the July heat.

The sun was behind the far peak, but it would be nearly bedtime before the light was gone.

J.J. sat up. "Feel," he said to her father and laid the older man's hand on her tummy. "It's a girl. The doctor let me listen to her heart. He gave us a picture of her. She looks weird."

Celia laughed as she stroked the hair away from J.J.'s forehead. "Just the way you looked inside your mommy," she told him.

"I did?"

She nodded.

"How do you know?" He clearly didn't want to believe this. "Did you see me?"

"No, but babies look that way—"

"I saw you," Hunter said. "You and your sister are as alike as two peas."

"But different pods," her father added, removing his hand when the baby stopped kicking.

A ripple of laughter went around the group.

Celia darted another glance at Hunter. He gave her an intense, sweeping perusal, his gaze running restlessly over her bosom, which had increased in size of late, and her rounded figure, before returning to his task at the grill. She sensed hunger in him. Her body responded hotly.

"Dinner's on," he called a moment later, removing the meat from the grill. "Stay put," he ordered when Celia started to rise. "You've done enough."

She'd baked cookies and pies and J.J.'s favorite cake earlier that week. Yesterday, before their guests had arrived, she'd gone to the grocery. Today, she'd prepared breakfast, a big lunch, then homemade dips and salads and her grandmother's slow-cooked molasses-flavored baked beans to go with chips and salsa for the cookout. The tomatoes and lettuce had come from her and J.J.'s garden.

Hunter settled J.J. on the steps with his plate and ordered the Lab off the patio. Tail dragging, the dog flopped down in the grass, dropped his head between his paws and sighed as if greatly insulted.

Everyone laughed in sympathy.

To Celia's surprise, Hunter fixed a plate and brought it to her, the hamburger prepared the way she liked it. He refilled her iced-tea glass before piling a plate high for himself. He sat on the planking next to her and leaned against the swing stand.

Celia caught her sister-in-law watching them, a thoughtful expression in her light blue eyes. Dawn smiled, as if pleased with the way things were going between them.

If only she knew, Celia thought tiredly. However, she returned the smile, then grimaced slightly as the baby stretched, punching out a noticeable bump in her side. Her hand automatically went toward the spot.

A large masculine hand covered the bump and pressed slightly to relieve the strain against her side.

Hunter seemed to know just how hard to push. When the bump shifted, he let up, then moved his hand slowly over her. The baby gave a few fluttery kicks, then settled down again. He removed his hand and began eating.

Her heart banged around uneasily. Longing rose again, closing her throat momentarily. She sipped the icy tea until she could resume eating.

After the meal, J.J. looked at her anxiously. Hunter raised his eyebrows. "Now?"

She nodded.

He and Dawn brought out the birthday presents. J.J.'s eyes glowed over twin rocket ships and a storybook that had sounds to go with it. He got a new cowboy hat and a lariat to practice his roping skills, plus a set of chaps to protect his legs from thorny bushes, and a building-block set that included propellers and wheels.

At Celia's prompting, J.J. remembered to thank each person for the gifts.

Hunter brought the birthday cake out, the candle flames fluttering like banners as he walked.

"Oh, neat!" J.J. said, his eyes wide. He raced over to the picnic table and climbed onto the bench on his knees.

Celia had painted a scene on the cake using different colors of frosting. There were mountains, a creek, barns and a boy on a pony waving his cowboy hat in the air while they rode like the wind.

Hunter touched her shoulder, then slipped his arms around her middle. She was at once acutely aware of his warmth in the narrow groove between her breasts and tummy.

The family gathered around and sang the birthday

song, then J.J. made a wish and blew out the candles. "It's the beautif'lest cake," he declared.

Celia moved from Hunter's unexpected embrace and cut the first piece. She gave it to J.J.

"Thank you," he said politely, then gave her a kiss.

She glanced at Hunter, but no emotion showed in his eyes. His smile was subdued and somehow sad. She gave him the next piece of cake before serving the rest.

"Where's Uncle Jackson?" she asked, her expression innocent as she looked around. "Well, he'll just miss out on the cake. We won't wait—"

A whinny interrupted her complaint. Jackson led a sturdy brown-and-white pony into sight from behind the house. Seeing the small crowd, the pony arched his neck and tossed his head as if leading a parade. Red ribbons with tiny bells were braided into the smoothly combed mane. On his back was a fancy saddle.

J.J. ran to the edge of the patio. "Is he—is he mine?" His gaze flew past her to land anxiously on his father's face.

Hunter nodded.

Dawn spoke up. "The pony is from your mommy and daddy. The saddle belonged to…" She frowned as she realized what she was saying.

"Mommy-April," Celia supplied, "when she was a little girl. Then it was Aunt Dawn's. She wanted you to have it. Uncle Jackson cleaned and polished it for you and did the ribbons and bells."

"He's the beautif'lest pony in the world," J.J. declared. It was love at first sight. He jumped from the patio and raced across the grass. He slowed before he got to the pony.

"Good boy," Jackson said as he approached the pony at a calmer pace.

J.J. patted his mount and let the pony sniff at him. The boy leaned forward, and they touched noses. Dawn snapped pictures of the event. The Lab, already used to the pony, waited for someone to throw his stick, then sank to the ground when no one paid him the slightest attention.

"Up you go," Jackson invited, standing aside. He gave J.J. a boost into the saddle.

While Celia worried and tried not to show it, the boy took the reins, clicked his tongue, and guided the pony across the lawn.

Hunter laid an arm around her shoulders. "He'll be okay. He knows how to handle a horse."

"A chip off the old block," Dawn bragged. "Takes after his mom and aunt." She immediately looked chagrined with herself at the second slip.

"April was a wonderful rider," Celia said firmly. "I showed J.J. the pictures of when she won the local barrel race when she was hardly more than his age."

"He's a fine, brave young man," her father declared.

"And polite, too," Kerri said.

"Celia has been good for him," Mrs. Ericson told them. "He stopped speaking for a long time, but somehow she brought him out of it."

All eyes turned on Celia.

"Oh, it wasn't what I did," she said, embarrassed. "He was talking, just not to… Uh, well, actually, he talked to his dog."

Hunter's grin was wry. "There have been times when I liked four-legged critters better than two-legged ones myself," he drawled.

The ripple of laughter broke the tension. Celia turned an anxious eye back to the little cowboy and his pony. Jackson was walking beside J.J., talking in his soft, calming manner as he coaxed boy and pony.

"I've asked Jackson to work with them," Hunter explained, tightening his arm around her in reassurance. "It'll be easier for J.J. to take instruction from him."

"And a hell of a lot easier on you." Her father grinned. "I tried to teach Celia, but the horse was too hard to control. It ran away with her. She fell off and broke her arm and collarbone."

"Ah," Hunter murmured close to her ear. "So that explains it."

She gave him an apologetic glance. "It was a long way to the ground."

"I'll find you a gentle mare." He patted her tummy. "Later. When you're ready."

"That might be never," she advised glumly.

Hunter and Dawn chuckled as if she were joking. But she thought she might be gone before she'd ever muster enough courage to get on a horse again.

"It's peaceful here. I see why you like it," her father said. It was early morning, the sun was just up. J.J. and Kerri were still asleep. Hunter, Jackson and the men were already at work. The haying season was under way.

Celia had discovered that meant a lot of extra work—cutting, drying, baling, hauling and storing.

The hay would grow and the work had to be done all over again, two or three times during the growing season. Hunter would come in, sweaty and tired each night. He went to bed early and rose before the sun came up.

"I've always loved the mountains," she murmured, lifting her hair away from her neck and letting the cool breeze caress her. In another hour, the sun would warm the valley and the men would shed their jackets, then their shirts as the work progressed.

She liked looking at her husband when he was stripped to the waist, his skin sun-bronzed and supple. Warmth swept through her. She had often wanted to run her hands over him when she saw him like that.

"I miss them," her father continued after a moment of comfortable silence. "But New York has been good to us. Kerri and I bought a place on Long Island. I hope you and your family can come visit when the baby is old enough."

"We will," she promised.

"Good—"

A childish treble cut off the rest of the statement. "Mommy, I'm hungry."

She waved to J.J., standing on the patio in his Batman pajamas, a black cape fluttering from his shoulders. "I'm being paged. I'll start breakfast."

"I'll stay out here for a few minutes."

She nodded and crossed the drive to the house. Scooping the barefoot boy into her arms, she tussled with him, kissing and tickling while they entered the house.

"Oh," she muttered. "I forgot to warn Grandpa about the stallion." She returned to the patio in time

to see her dad stop by the paddock fence. "Dad, look
out—"

Too late.

The stallion stuck his head over the top railing. Her
father reached up to pat him.

"No!" she yelled out the open door.

The stud bared his teeth and lunged.

Mr. Campbell drew his hand back. The stallion bit
into the front of his shirt. She heard her father utter
a startled curse. The horse struck again, this time getting the forearm. Celia put J.J. down and ran toward
the paddock.

"Hunter!" she screamed, hoping he was close by.

He and Jackson came out of the stable together.

Her father stumbled backward and fell to the
ground. The stallion turned and kicked the fence. The
top rail flew off. He whirled, raced away, turned and
came back.

Celia realized the beast was going to take the fence
and that he would trample her father when he did.
"Dad, move!"

Mr. Campbell rolled to the side just as the horse
sailed over the fence railing and pounded up the road.
Hunter ran in front of the stallion and turned him to
the side. Jackson emerged from the tack room and
tossed a lariat to Hunter. He kept one for himself.
They headed up the road.

The stallion paused in the yard. Celia realized he
was looking her way—and that J.J. had followed her
outside. She turned and ran toward the boy.

Her heart pounded with the beat of the hooves behind her. She grabbed J.J.'s hand and ran as hard as
she could. She heard shouts as Hunter and Jackson

yelled. She couldn't hear the words, and she didn't stop to listen.

She and J.J. reached the patio, then the kitchen. She had the door closed by the time the stallion reared at the patio steps and spun around to face the men. Twin ropes floated over his head and closed around his neck.

The stallion screamed and lashed out in rage.

A third rope enclosed him as one of the hands joined in the fray. Between them, the three men subdued the horse and got him back into the stable.

Her hands shaking, Celia tossed ice cubes into a plastic bag, zipped it closed and went to her father. He was walking toward the house, his arm pressed to his stomach. She met him at the steps and helped him into the kitchen.

"Sit there," she said. She unfastened his shirt and peeled it off. An angry bruise had already formed on his abdomen. Red marks outlined the bite on his forearm. "Put this on your stomach."

She gave him the ice pack while she examined his arm. The skin wasn't broken. She made up another bag of ice and laid it over the teeth imprints.

"What happened?" Kerri asked. She was in her robe, her hair still tousled from sleep. "I heard a terrible commotion outside— Hugh, you're hurt!"

He grinned. "I got too close to an unfriendly horse. Man, he can bite. I'm fine," he assured his wife when she rushed over to him. He let her see the wounds.

"I'll have breakfast in a minute," Celia told them, bringing coffee to the table. She gave J.J. a bowl of his favorite cereal while she cooked omelets for the adults.

Anger sizzled in her as she heated ham slices. It roiled through her as she flipped the omelets. By the time she heard Hunter's steps on the patio, she was furious.

So was he.

He strode into the kitchen like a Titan bent on destruction. He gave her father a swift check, then turned on her. "Don't ever run from an animal again," he ordered.

Deathly quiet fell over the room.

"What was I supposed to do—stand there and let him run us down?" she demanded, incredulous at the attack.

"You face him. You yell and wave your arms and flap your shirt at him. You *don't* run."

"You can stand there and get run over by that maniac horse, but *I'm* not. That stallion is dangerous—"

Hunter leaned close, his nose inches from hers. "He's only dangerous if you let him get the upper hand."

"You mean the upper hoof?" she suggested. "What do I do if he kicks me—roll over and play dead?"

His fury flamed over her, leaving her hot-faced in front of their relatives. "You don't act stupid. J.J. shows better sense than you do around animals."

She had no retort for that. "They scare me," she said, her voice dropping to a quiet note of confession.

Hunter hesitated, then spun and walked out.

After another beat of silence, she took a deep breath, then smiled. "Well, I think these are ready."

She took up the omelets, served the cantaloupe she'd sliced earlier and added a bowl of toasted English muffins to the fare. She took her seat, ignoring the conspicuous absence of the host.

"So you're off to your friends' up in Oregon?" she asked her stepmother. "Didn't you say they had orchards?"

For the rest of the meal, they chatted about the charms of Oregon pear and apple orchards. After Kerri helped with the cleaning up, she and Celia's father gathered their luggage and jackets.

At the car, her dad paused, his hands on her shoulders. Celia tensed for some well-meaning advice.

"Take care, baby," he said, sympathy in his eyes.

"I will," she chirruped, sounding like a perky robin.

But when the car disappeared from sight on the winding ranch road, she felt as if someone had pulled the pin and let all her air out. She gazed at the paddock where the stallion now grazed as peacefully as a lamb.

"Devil horse," she said.

He seemed to embody everything wrong with her marriage—her fears and worries for her child, her restless days and lonely nights. Returning to the house, she glanced at all the shining surfaces, at the plants, the bright points of color she'd added. All at once, it all seemed futile.

J.J. played quietly with his connector set, busy with the spaceship he was building. Her eyes filled with tears. She rushed down the hallway to her room.

With the door safely closed, she lay on the bed and curled into a ball. She pressed her hands over her face, afraid to give in to the misery that sapped her, afraid that once she started, she wouldn't be able to quit.

She stiffened when the door opened.

J.J. came to her and put his arms around her neck. "Don't cry," he whispered. "I love you. Don't cry."

"I'm not crying," she murmured. She laughed to show him she was fine.

Sitting up, she held him close, taking comfort in the wiry warmth of his little-boy embrace. He was kinder than his father—

To her dismay, tears spurted from her eyes, then poured like a burst fountain down her face.

"Don't," J.J. implored. "Don't cry." He wiped at her face with his hands.

She tried to laugh, to show him she was fine, but the tears defeated her. She choked and gasped and finally buried her face in his neck so he wouldn't see until she got a grip on herself.

"It's okay," she managed to reassure him. "I'm just…fine…really…."

He squirmed from her arms and raced out the door. She heard a door close and guessed he'd gone to his room. She had things to do—lunch to prepare for the men, shopping that afternoon. But she didn't move.

Hunter stopped and looked at the blister in annoyance. He'd mucked out the stalls without wearing gloves, but the blister offended him nonetheless. He looked up when J.J. entered the open door at the end of the stable. The boy stopped in front of him, his expression worried.

"Mommy's crying," he announced and crossed his stick-thin arms over his chest. He glared up at Hunter.

Hunter's heart gave a hitch. He ignored it. He didn't need a lecture from that unreliable organ any more than he did from his son. "Women do that. Often."

J.J.'s chin jutted out. "You made her sad."

"And now I suppose you think I should make her happy?" he snapped, hiding his guilt behind the anger.

The boy nodded emphatically, not backing down an inch.

Hunter frowned at his son.

J.J. frowned back.

Sticking the pitchfork in its usual place, Hunter considered his options. "Tell you what. Let's ask Aunt Dawn to let you have lunch with her. I'll take…Mommy to town for a surprise and treat her to lunch. You think she'd like that?"

"I guess."

Hunter clasped his son's shoulder. "Come on. Let's get moving. I'll take care of Mommy." It was easier to say the word the second time. It didn't come naturally, as it had with April, but it was easier.

He took J.J. to Dawn's and explained that he and Celia needed to go to town. He'd hardly gotten out the door when he heard his son tell Dawn his dad had made his mommy cry. He was sure Dawn would soon have the whole story.

At the house, he paused and took off his boots at the door. The place seemed unusually quiet. A troubling sensation attacked his chest. Maybe he had been a little rough, but it had scared him to see Celia and J.J. running, the stallion pawing the air before charging after them.

He walked down the hall and stopped at her bedroom. The door was open. Celia sat on the bed, staring at her feet.

When she looked up, there was no smile and none of the bright anticipation of life he'd come to expect from her. A hint of confusion crossed her face.

"Is it time for lunch?" She glanced at the clock.

"No, it's early yet." He cleared his throat. "I guess it's time for an apology. I'm sorry for yelling at you—"

"Don't." She held up both hands as if warding off a blow. "You were right. I didn't think."

He got a good look at her eyes and saw the spiky lashes, damp from her tears. She quickly lowered her head, as if ashamed. A lump formed in his throat.

"Hell," he said, "I feel like crying myself." He sat beside her and dropped an arm around her shoulders.

The stiffness in her body told of her resistance to his presence. She didn't want him in her room, touching her. It suddenly became imperative that he did.

"I was wrong to yell at you. Most people do run when something is chasing them. It's a natural reaction. The problem is, animals chase things that run from them."

He looped a strand of hair that had escaped her ponytail behind her ear, then lingered to explore the softness of her skin. He massaged her neck, then her shoulders until the rigidity left her body.

"I should start lunch," she said. She rubbed her eyes, brushing away the last of the moisture that clung to her lashes, then edged away from him.

"I thought we'd go to town," he told her. "The men can fend for themselves."

"I don't feel like it." She stood, and he let her go. He trailed behind her, then insisted on helping with the noon meal. She set him to peeling potatoes while she prepared oven-fried chicken.

"You're a good cook," he said when the silence had stretched longer than he could stand.

"Thank you."

"Did your mother teach you?"

She shrugged. "I helped her and my grandmother when I was a kid. I've never considered it difficult to do."

"A natural," he murmured. "In many ways."

He covertly watched her move around the kitchen, her hands sure and skilled as she worked. She wore her usual shorts and matching top, her feet in soft-soled sandals. Her tummy, far from being unattractive to him, was interestingly rounded. With his child.

Heat stirred in him, surprising him as it always did. That she had the ability to excite him when no other woman had, was a jarring revelation. It had to mean something.

What? That was the question.

He watched her mix up corn bread and pour it into a hot skillet. Her fingers were short, the nails rosy with health. She buffed them instead of wearing polish. He had accepted that they were the hands that had caressed him in those images he couldn't quite grasp, yet which still haunted him.

His gaze traveled down her legs. Her ankles hadn't puffed up yet. Even when they did, her legs were shapely, forming an attractive V where the calf muscle attached to the Achilles tendon. Her feet were small, the toes delicate. Her thighs were firm, tapering sexily to her knees.

He became aware of her stillness and glanced up to meet her eyes. She was watching him, her face flushed, as he perused her body.

Rising, he walked slowly toward her until he stood close enough to touch. Her pupils expanded when she realized what was on his mind. She stiffened when he laid his hands on her shoulders.

"Don't be afraid," he said. He didn't want to frighten her. He'd never meant to do that. Not ever.

"I'm not."

He smiled slightly at her valiant denial, then settled his mouth over hers, a brushstroke of pleasure. "Liar."

She turned her head. "What are you doing?"

"Making love to my beautiful wife."

The words surprised him as much as they did her. He didn't know where they came from, only that they felt right. At this moment, everything felt right. He rubbed his hands along her arms, soothing her, getting her used to his touch.

It came to him, then. If their marriage was to succeed, they each had to work at it, including him. So he'd start with the courtship they'd never had. He didn't know if he could do more, but for now, he could kiss and hold her. That would be enough for the present. Later, after the baby was born, maybe there would be more.

"We'll take each day as it comes," he murmured, lifting his head so he could see her expression.

He saw by the darkening of her eyes that she understood what he meant. That was what she had tried to tell him when they were first married, but he'd been too stunned and too stubborn to see it. He would try to do as she'd suggested—treat each other with kindness.

Bending slightly, he touched her lips again. They trembled under his. Hunger gnawed at his insides. He pulled her closer, then closer still, nestling her against him, fitting his body to accommodate hers. He took the kiss deeper—

A commotion on the patio heralded the arrival of the hands for the noon meal.

Tom was the first in. "Well, looks like the boss is having dessert before we even get to eat. That don't seem fair to me."

Hunter lifted his head, but held Celia when she would have moved away. "Better sit down, boys. If Tom's stomach is as big as his mouth, the rest of us won't get much if we don't grab it now."

He helped his wife put the meal on the table. Each time he brushed against her, her breath quickened. At least she was as aware of him as he was of her. That was a start.

"You guys are on your own tonight," he announced. "I'm taking my wife out to dinner."

Celia looked surprised, then pleased.

Hunter watched her closely…. Yes, there it was— the light shyly dawning in her eyes, making them gleam with that bright expectancy she always seemed to have of life. He relaxed. Things would be different in the future, he vowed. He would make her feel wanted….

Chapter Twelve

Celia gratefully accepted Hunter's arm when they stepped up on the patio. He had taken her to the restaurant by the lake for dinner after settling J.J. with Dawn and Jackson for the night. However, she was aware of the emptiness of the house as they started inside.

Without J.J. as a shield between them, she felt alone and vulnerable to Hunter's charm. He had been charming all afternoon—to make up for having yelled at her.

He'd even insisted she dance a couple of slow numbers after they finished their meal. For the first minute, she'd felt awkward. After that, she'd relaxed and let Hunter guide her into a series of intricate steps.

It was something she'd always loved—dancing

with him. He was one of the few men she'd ever
known who enjoyed dancing and was really good at
it. But after the second dance, he'd looked at her
swollen ankles, apologized, then driven them home.

"Wait," he said at the door.

She glanced up at him to see what was the problem.
His mouth came down on hers, taking her by surprise.
She turned her face and laughed nervously. "What
are we doing?"

"I'm getting my good-night kiss," he murmured
huskily. He ran his hands inside her jacket and along
her back. "I've been thinking about it all the way
home."

She stopped smiling when he lifted her face to his
and brushed across her lip with his thumb, then with
his tongue. When he covered her mouth again, she
was ready. She strained upward, longing washing out
sense as she clung to his shoulders and wished for
things that would never be.

When he lifted his head, they were both breathing
hard.

He smiled, then chucked her under the chin. "That
was fun. Let's make a date for next week. Same time,
same place?"

She nodded, thinking she must be dreaming because Hunter seemed to be coming on to her. She
shook her head slightly and hurried to her room.

A few minutes later, in bed with her feet propped
on a pillow, she relived the evening. Like a teenager
after her first big date. For some reason, that made
her feel sad.

She went to sleep, but woke at the first strike of
lightning and roll of thunder across the sky. The day

had been hot and muggy, the air sullen and still. The clouds had been gathering over the near peaks all afternoon. She wasn't surprised by the storm.

Sitting up, she hugged her knees as close as she could and waited for the tempest to pass.

"Celia?"

She faced the door. "Yes?"

Hunter entered the room. "I heard the storm and wondered if you were awake."

By the dim glow of the night-light, she could see he wore white briefs. The rest of his body looked dark and mysterious, with enticing hollows and planes to explore. "Yes. It woke me a few minutes ago."

His weight depressed the mattress. She scooted over, giving him room beside her. He slipped under the covers and stretched his legs out next to hers. His feet touched the pillow and he fished it out. "What's this?"

She explained its use.

To her amazement, he moved down the bed until he could reach her feet. He rubbed and massaged until she was nearly swooning in ecstasy. Ripples of electricity cavorted up her legs and lodged deep inside her.

"I... That's fine now," she murmured, unable to stand his touch any longer.

He caressed her legs, lingering to massage her calves for a moment, then moving to the backs of her knees. He paused and stroked the skin there. Under his guidance on New Year's Eve, she'd discovered that was a very sensitive spot. Seven months later, it still was.

When he moved up beside her, she sighed in relief.

It didn't last long. His hand dropped onto her thigh, slipping beneath her nightshirt to stroke her bare skin.

She tensed.

"Easy," he murmured. "Is it okay for me to touch you for a while?"

"Why?" Her voice quivered a little.

"It feels nice."

"Oh." She couldn't think of another word to add to that profound statement.

His chuckle fanned the hair at her temple. She ran her fingers through the strands to smooth the tangles. Heat radiated from his big masculine body as he moved closer. He put an arm around her while continuing to stroke with his free hand.

"You have the smoothest skin, as soft as J.J.'s."

"It's vitamin E. I take one every day and it's in my lotion, too."

"Is it?" He laughed again.

The sound dipped right down inside her, making her hot and sort of melty inside. "Yes." She clasped her fingers together over her tummy and wondered what was happening.

His chest hair tickled her arm. She wanted to turn to him and run her fingers over his skin, but she didn't. He wasn't going to stay the night.

Maybe this was his way of accepting her. Maybe it would work...when he got used to having *her* for a wife, rather than the woman he wanted and couldn't have.

Her heart picked up its beat. Heat seared her insides to cinders. She wanted him to go, to stay; to stop...to stay....

The lightning flashed and struck earth.

Celia let out an involuntary cry. Hunter enclosed her in his arms and made shushing noises. She lifted a hand and touched him then, unable to hold in the need.

The acrid smell of burned wood blew in on the stiff breeze that flung the sheers outward like banners, then sucked them back against the screen. With it came the fresh ozone scent of the storm as it hunkered down over the valley. Lightning again split the sky, and thunder reverberated in the hills. She shivered.

"The storm will probably last the rest of the night," Hunter told her. "Would you like to sleep in my room?"

The question was so foreign to anything she'd expected from him that it took her several seconds to interpret it.

"In your bed?" she asked finally, still not sure what he meant and cautious about taking anything for granted.

"Yes."

"I… All right. I guess."

He swung out of bed and lifted her into his arms. In five seconds, she was tucked under his covers.

She had another glimpse of long masculine legs before he slipped in beside her. He bunched the pillows behind his head and pulled her into the curve of his left side. Together they watched the storm.

The curtains fluttered in the wind as the ones in her room did. From here, she could see the barn and stables and paddocks. Beyond those, the fields of alfalfa and oats heaved like ocean swells. A horse neighed nervously.

"Has lightning ever hit the barn?" she asked.

"Several times. We have deflectors on all the buildings. They can take a pretty hard jolt."

She wondered if she could, as current flowed into her at an increasing rate from his fingers, which were rubbing back and forth on her arm. "We'd better go to sleep. The morning comes early out here."

"We won't be doing hay tomorrow," he replied. "It'll be raining."

He shifted his thigh against hers. The muscles flexed like woven cables, hard as steel beneath his skin.

"It's hot—" she began and stopped abruptly.

"Yes," he murmured. His lips touched her hair, then her forehead. "Give me your mouth."

She hesitated. If she gave him that much, what more would he want? Her heart? He already had that. So what was she leery of?

"Don't be afraid," he coaxed.

"Do you read minds?" she asked and automatically smiled to ward off his taking her too seriously.

He stroked her lips with the tips of his fingers, setting off wildfires there to join the bolts of lightning running under her skin. "I can read your hesitancy." He paused for a long, thoughtful moment. "Actually, I'm taking your advice. Let's pull together, Celia, and see if we can make this marriage work—for our sakes as well as for our children's."

With the gentlest of pressure, he touched her abdomen, then splayed his hand over her.

"Do you think we can?" She bit down on her lip as the question spilled out from the caution hardlearned so long ago from people she'd loved.

"If we try. We can try, can't we?"

She thought it over while his hand played havoc with her senses. When he cupped her breast, she nearly groaned.

"Can't we?" he whispered, kissing along her temple.

There was no way she could hold out when he was being gentle and outrageous and teasing, the way he'd been on New Year's when he'd taken her passion and her heart completely.

"Yes."

His mouth swooped down on hers, surprising her into a gasp. He claimed advantage at once, sweeping inside and making the kiss deep and intimate.

Need rose so fierce and terrible, she couldn't deny it, either. She raked her fingers into his hair and pulled him closer, answering every thrust of his tongue with one of her own. Their lips blended, parted, murmured words that made no sense; met again, harder, deeper, going hot and hotter until their two bodies became incandescent like pottery in a kiln, caught in the same glow with no boundaries between them.

"I want you," she sobbed at one point. "Now. Now, oh, now, oh, please." And she thought she might die from the terrible ache of needing.

His lips moved over her—here, there, tasting, testing, claiming her passion for his own, driving her mindless as her need became more demanding.

"Yes," he told her. "Good… You're doing…so good. Take what you want. Take it all…."

The wind riffled the curtains. The storm was in the room, in his stroking hands, in his mouth that moved over her relentlessly, wild the way the storm was wild.

She gave a keening cry as he drove the lightning into her with each flickering caress he bestowed.

"Take it," he coaxed hoarsely. "Take all you want."

The storm was in her, pulsing with unleashed energy, tearing caution asunder with savage abandon, finding voice through her as she shrieked and moaned and lost herself in his arms.

"Oh, love, oh, love," she cried as the tempest exploded in her, lifting her into the swirling clouds of release, dissolving into a torrent.

Rain hit the window with a resounding force.

Hunter wiped the tears from her face, his expression solemn as he watched her come down from that nameless peak where passion ruled. She lowered her lashes, not sure what she had given away during those moments of ecstasy.

"I want to come in you," he said. "For a while." He waited for her consent.

Something tender opened in her as she suddenly saw his hesitancy, his own uncertainty about the outcome of this tryst. It had never occurred to her that a man could be as vulnerable as a woman in this area. She nodded, a ridiculous shyness coming over her.

He knelt between her thighs and stroked her intimately, then positioned himself. Slowly, with exquisite patience, he moved until their bodies had merged. Aftershocks of passion trembled through her. Still caressing her, he began to move, slowly at first, then faster as she responded, rolling her hips toward him each time he thrust forward.

Carefully, he drew her legs up and over his shoulders. Her eyes widened as new tremors of delight cascaded over her taut nerves. He smiled slightly, breathing hard now, moving in deep, deep strokes that funneled her attention to that one spot, the place where they touched most intimately.

The storm rolled in again, not quite so harshly, not quite so greedy this time. She let it build, felt the moment when it went out of control, knew when Hunter went beyond the point of stopping. Time slowed and quickened, slowed and quickened, then—

She cried out. His hoarse groan followed in almost the same breath. They moved together until the last drop of passion was wrung from the moment.

He rested over her, his weight on his elbows, their bellies touching. The child moved and stretched, then became quiet again.

Celia opened her eyes. Hunter was watching her. She waited to see what he would say. A moment went by, then he smiled. "That was good. Very, very good."

Hunter woke to an unfamiliar sensation. A small, soft body was tucked into his, a feminine tush snuggled against his groin. A flash of joy lit up his soul; then he realized the woman in his bed wasn't the one...

He backed off from that thought and memories of the past it brought forth. Instead, he studied the face of the woman who was now his wife. Her expression was as young and innocent as J.J.'s in sleep. Remembering the night and the wild, urgent, desperate lovemaking he'd engaged in with her, he experienced a rush of gratitude. And confusion.

Why her?

He'd dated more sophisticated women, women who were much more poised, beautiful and experienced than Celia, women who should have turned him on if anyone could. Why hadn't they?

His slumbering wife reminded him of a waif at times. Her smile was valiant even when her eyes held that crushed look that made him feel like a heel for berating her.

He shook his head in wonder, not sure where their marriage was going, but knowing that somehow they had crossed a bridge—or maybe it was only a stepping-stone. At any rate, it was a beginning.

The rain beat against the roof with a soft patter. It would be a lazy day. Other than tending the stock, work would have to wait.

He planted a kiss in the delectable hollow where her neck met her shoulder and breathed deeply of her womanly scent. His body stirred hungrily.

She opened her eyes.

"Hi," he said. He chuckled at her startled, round-eyed expression, as if she couldn't figure out how she got there.

Along with the stirring of passion, a sense of peace seeped into his consciousness. He realized he'd slept well for the first time in years. He nuzzled her neck again.

"Do you feel as good as I do this morning?" he asked, giving her an oblique kind of glance that he'd once heard a woman describe as sexy. He paused to analyze why he wanted to be sexy for this woman, then gave it up.

When she stared at him in amazement, he grinned, liking the sense of play between them. Her smile flashed a little uncertainly, but her eyes became mischievous.

"Do men always crow like roosters over something as simple as sex?" she asked, taking up the sensual gambit.

"Yes." He rubbed his chin thoughtfully. "I seem to recall you were doing quite a bit of cackling last night yourself."

It was interesting to watch a woman blush, to see the sweep of pink travel up her chest and neck into her face.

She patted back a yawn and stretched. "I'll start breakfast. I'm hungry this morning."

"Me, too. Trying to keep up with a wild woman in bed can sure wear a man down."

With an indignant huff, she crawled out of the sack, then realized she was nude. She made a grab for the sheet. He tugged it out of her hand and joined her on the rug beside the bed.

"You don't have to be shy in front of me. A pregnant woman is an interesting sight. As your husband, I'm fascinated by the process." He turned her toward the bathroom. "Have you ever showered with a man?"

At her quick shake of the head, he gently pushed her in front of him and into the shower.

"Then we have another interesting experience in front of us this morning. And maybe another after that."

He adjusted the water, then took turns using the soap with her. Later, after they had eaten eggs and toast, he guided her back to bed. To his relief, his reactions were the same as during the night. For some reason, he could now make love to this woman when he hadn't been able to with any other. He wasn't going to question miracles.

Celia pressed her hands against her back and massaged the achy muscles. She was starting the eighth month of her pregnancy and had gained over twenty pounds. The doctor had taken her off salt because of the swelling. It didn't matter. The temperature had soared, and she didn't feel like eating anyway.

But she did feel happy. Sort of.

She had moved her clothing into Hunter's room, although she'd left her computer in the guest room. J.J. had noticed and commented on the change. Hunter had told his son it was time and left it at that. J.J. had been satisfied.

There was, within her soul, a wistful yearning for things she'd never found—for that tender, fierce, shining love she'd glimpsed at times between Dawn and Jackson—but she didn't let herself expect them.

An article in a popular women's magazine had advised that as long as a man had good food, hot sex and a comfortable bed, he would be content. She didn't know about that, but she did feel that as long as people were honest and faithful and decent to each other, affection could grow in a marriage. That was what she was counting on.

She and Hunter had been living truly as husband and wife for two weeks. He was a careful and charming lover, gentle with her, making sure she was pleased before taking his own pleasure.

That puzzled him—that he took pleasure in her when he hadn't been able to before. It puzzled her, too. Sometimes in the evening, she'd find him watching her, unconscious that he did so, as if looking for clues.

He always came in for lunch before the men, using the time to help her set the table. His step seemed eager when he crossed the patio and entered the room, but in his eyes were the questions, always the questions, about them.

She couldn't give him answers. She could only offer her lips when he turned her face to his for a stolen kiss before the cowboys clambered into the house, or her arms when he turned to her each night, as hungry for her caresses as she was for his. He didn't love her, but there was need. And that seemed to bother him.

Sighing, she gathered up the container of brownies and the jug of lemonade and went outside. Her clothing stuck to her as sweat popped out. It was hot, it was August, and the hay cutting and baling were in full swing.

J.J. and Lab were sitting in the shade under the oak tree. J.J. was flying one of his connector-set space fighters. He'd already eaten the brownie she'd given to him. His cup of lemonade was on the grass.

Jackson was in the paddock with the "devil" horse. He'd put covers over the stallion's hooves and a muzzle over his mouth. The stud was excited.

Celia could see the frequent rippling under his skin as he scented the mare in the stable. The stallion wheeled when Celia passed on the road, his eyes rolling in their sockets, showing white as he watched her pass. He trumpeted a challenge, startling her.

She hurried on and went to the alfalfa field. Tom and Hunter were working together—Tom baling,

Hunter driving a device that lifted and stacked the bales that would go into the barn. The overflow was formed into giant rolls, each weighing half a ton and left outside for the winter.

Hunter turned off the stacker when he saw her stop by the field and wave her arm. He jumped down and ambled over to her with a long-legged stride that caused a hitch in her breathing. His hair had lightened with golden brown streaks and his eyes seemed to shine in the deep tan of his face.

Sweaty and sun-bronzed, with his unbuttoned shirt fluttering behind him as he moved, he was incredibly handsome in her eyes. He smiled when he stopped beside her.

"I hope that's something delicious to eat," he said, giving her a sexy once-over.

She wondered if he truly thought she was attractive, or if he was just sex-starved after his years of loneliness. Although their lives seemed to be meshing nicely now, she worried about him.

On New Year's Eve, he'd been so lonely and empty inside. He had thought his life was settled when he'd married April. He'd found everything he'd ever wanted with her, and then it was gone. Life was like that. She knew. It set a person up, then turned on you, tearing your soul apart.

Celia opened the plastic container. "Brownies by request, sir," she said brightly.

"Hey, Tom, here're those brownies you were hinting so strongly about the other night," he called to his fellow worker, who had seen her and turned off his machine, too.

Tom loped toward them, a grin cutting through the

dust on his face. "Ooo-wee!" he exclaimed. "You're about the prettiest sight a man could see on a day like this."

The men helped themselves to paper cups of lemonade and a big square of the snack. She'd learned to divide treats into pieces two to four times the size she would normally use with her schoolteacher friends. Cowboys ate as if they were all first cousins to Paul Bunyan.

"How's it going?" She surveyed the sixty-acre field.

"Okay," Hunter said. "We'll work until dark, maybe longer. There's another storm brewing and we need to get this cutting in the barn."

She'd learned that hay could rot on the ground if it stayed wet too long; that a hard rain could knock all the leaves off or the leaves could crumple if the hay got too dry, leaving only stems for the cattle to feed on during the winter. When hay came "in order," it was neither too wet nor too dry but just right to bale. That was when the men worked long, hard hours.

"Do you want me to bring supper out to you?"

Hunter motioned for her to join him and walked over to the shade where Tom rested while he ate. "Could you grill hamburgers? The men like them, and they're quick to eat."

"Of course."

He polished off the brownie and the last slug of lemonade, then refilled the cup and drank that down with hardly a pause. He swiped his mouth with the back of his hand, then leaned over to her.

Instead of the quick kiss she'd expected, he whispered for her hearing only, "You're damn agreeable since I got you in my bed."

His grin slashed a white line across his face as her eyes widened at his sexy teasing.

"Maybe I'll stay that way—as long as you keep me happy there," she retorted. "Tom, you want another serving?"

Hunter watched her sashay over to the old cowboy. He enjoyed the view when she bent down so Tom could make his selection. He also liked the way she teased with him. She was growing more secure in their relationship. Not quite at ease, but more comfortable.

For some reason it had become important that she be at ease with him the way she was with his son. J.J. had accepted her completely in his life. That was good for her as well as for the child. And for himself?

Hunter tore his gaze away from her shapely legs and looked at the clouds gathering on the peaks west of them.

For himself, he didn't know. There was an increasing urgency to get to the house each evening. For the first time in years, he looked forward to quitting work and having a quiet evening. And there was the sex. But was that all?

He didn't want to be drawn into love's subtle net of needs and expectations. He'd been there, done that and had come out the other end empty and dead inside.

And yet… He glanced over to where Celia chatted with Tom about the haying operation. Sometimes, when he was inside her, when passion was high and he forgot the past, then…then he felt something more than lust or gratitude for this woman he'd married so precipitously.

A distant rumble reminded him that nature had her own whims. "Yo, old man, there's work to be done."

Tom roused from some long-winded tale that brought the sparkle to Celia's eyes. When she turned to him, a laugh on her rosebud mouth, his heart seized up and wouldn't let go.

He put a hand to his chest, shocked by the sudden pain. It was like the moment when he'd realized April wasn't going to open her eyes and wrinkle her nose at him and call him "silly" in her special way that meant she thought he was wonderful.

Spinning away from Celia and her smile, he fought the pain. He'd known he would never again experience that crazy, rapturous feeling he'd had when he'd been in love, but he'd also assumed he wouldn't have the searing pain that indicated a need so great, it cut into his soul.

He headed for the stacker and the calming effect of work, aware of his wife's eyes following him as he fled.

Chapter Thirteen

Celia walked toward the house, her head down, her eyes on the road in front of her. Something had happened. Hunter had been playful at first, then he'd turned introspective. For a second she'd witnessed the bleakness in his eyes again. Had she caused it?

Women always thought like that, she reminded herself. As if they were responsible for fixing the world, for making everybody happy. A man, as much as a woman, had to be responsible for his own well-being. It wasn't fair to expect someone else to do it.

Not that Hunter had asked.

He'd never asked for anything from her. He accepted her passion and gave it back tenfold. He appreciated her cooking and her care of his home and son. He'd told her that. But those were the only places their lives crossed.

She laid a protective hand over her waist and sighed. Mood swings were to be expected at this stage of her pregnancy. The books said it was normal to feel clumsy and big. Well, she was both of those. And achy, too.

"Celia, stay back."

She stopped and looked toward the stable.

Jackson was using his weight on the lead rope to hold the stallion. The devil horse was acting up, as usual—teeth bared, ears back, hooves flashing as he tried to rear up.

The breeding session must be over for the day. She hoped the poor mare had gotten more out of it than a bite on the neck.

Because of this one horse, Jackson's black stallion and Dawn's silver mare had been moved permanently to the Ericson place. The remuda mares had been moved to a far pasture. Celia had seen the stud bite a plug out of a friendly old cow-pony's ear when he came too near.

She stood still until Jackson had moved on down the gravel road, leading the horse to another field to graze.

J.J. landed his rocket ship on the Lab's thick coat, making noises that represented the cutting back of engines.

Joining him, Celia built a rocket ship and zoomed it around his head and crashed it on his tickle spot.

"Ready for a nap?"

J.J. shook his head.

"Five minutes."

"Ten." He loved to bargain.

They settled on eight. She gave him a countdown.

"Five minutes," she said. "Two minutes." She watched the time. "Ten, nine, eight, seven, six..."

J.J. stood and joined in. "Five, four, three, two, one. Blast off." He zoomed his rocket into the air.

They walked to the house together. The Lab followed and flopped down in the shade under the patio steps to snooze until J.J. reappeared.

After washing up and talking to the boy for a few minutes, Celia kissed his forehead and left him. She stretched out on the sofa, her feet propped on the armrest, and went to sleep.

She didn't know what woke her. She opened her eyes and listened. The house was quiet. Too quiet. She got up and padded down the hallway.

J.J.'s room was empty.

After pulling on her sandals, she went outside. The Lab was gone, so he and J.J. were off on an adventure. She shaded her eyes and glanced toward the oak tree. Not there.

"J.J.!" she called.

No answer.

Had he gone to join his father in the field? He liked to sit in Hunter's lap and help guide the tractor. Or maybe over to Dawn's or his grandmother's house?

He was very good about letting her know where he was going, but he was only a child. He might have forgotten. She turned to go inside and call the other women when she saw him come out of the stable. He had his pony in tow. The Lab pranced around them.

She joined the trio by the fence. "Hi, shall I saddle Herc for you?"

Herc was short for Hercules. The pony, although a

gelding, thought he was king of the mountain around the ranch and let the other geldings know it when he was in the pasture. He got the juiciest grazing spot and the best dust hollow, or else he annoyed the others until they moved.

"Yes. He wants to go for a ride."

"Yeah, I know who wants to go for a ride."

She glanced around, but didn't see Jackson or Dawn. Hunter and Tom were on the far side of the sixty-acre field. The cowboys were in the mountains, riding fences and checking cattle. She would have preferred that one of them be close by.

She saddled the pony with J.J.'s helpful advice. "Need a leg up?" she asked, ignoring the pings of anxiety that vibrated through her. Honestly, the pony was a safe mount and J.J. had ridden him dozens of times before.

But always with his father or uncle or aunt nearby.

He put his foot into her clasped hands and swung into the saddle with the ease of a rodeo rider. She stepped to the side. "No farther than the first curve."

"Okay."

She settled down under the oak tree and kept an eye on her stepson. Idly plucking the grass beside her knee, she let her mind drift into a hazy, nonthinking mode. A bumblebee, heavy with pollen, cruised past her, his body looking way too big for his fragile wings.

Once she'd read that bumblebees shouldn't be able to fly. But they did. She smiled. So, miracles could happen.

She considered her situation. Maybe it hadn't been such a bad idea to ask Hunter for a child on New

Year's Eve. She had a husband she loved, a son she adored and a baby she could hardly wait to hold. She lived in a nice house in the country. There were worse things—

A shrill scream rang out and echoed off the mountains that surrounded the valley. Fear bolted through her. She gazed all about but didn't see anything alarming. Then her eyes went to J.J. as he U-turned at the curve in the road and headed toward her.

He waved and urged the pony into a trot, then a canter.

She bit back the need to tell him to slow down, to be careful, to hold on tight.

The savage scream erupted again.

Celia surveyed the near paddocks. The studhorse wasn't visible in any of them.

J.J. stopped the pony halfway down the road and stared past her, fear on his face.

She whipped around.

The stallion sailed over a stock fence, galloped toward them, then stopped no more than fifty yards away from her, shook his head and stamped his front hooves.

Resisting the urge to run, Celia gauged the distance to the house. It was a hundred feet and formed the third point in a triangle with her and the horse, but she knew she had no chance of getting there.

The brute uttered several throaty challenges, then stamped some more when she didn't move.

Grabbing the hem of her full maternity top, Celia lifted her arms slowly into the air as if she were a ballerina performing an intricate movement. The top rippled in the warm breeze, forming bat wings at each side of her.

Don't run. Make yourself look bigger. Yell.

Her first sound came out as a croak. She cleared her throat and tried again. "Hai-i-i," she yelled and waved her arms to and fro so the material frothed around her.

She heard hooves behind her.

The stallion threw up his head and trumpeted. The pony whickered a brazen reply and, neck outstretched, headed straight for the bigger horse.

"Get away!" J.J. shouted at the brute.

"No!" she cried. "J.J., no!"

From the corner of her eye, she saw the stud rear, then come down on all fours. Teeth bared, he headed for the boy and the pony. The Lab barked and frolicked around them.

Rational thought left her. She ran on instinct now, straight into the path of the stallion. She screamed as loud as she could. "Get! Get back! Get out of here!"

The horse veered to the side, reared and spun in a tight circle. He gave her a malicious once-over.

Celia stood fifty feet away and stared him straight in the eye, her top held out like batwings.

J.J. sawed on the reins and the pony stopped about ten feet from her. She heard the air rasping in her throat as she tried to think.

A standoff. What now? She didn't dare back down.

The pony shook his head. The bridle jingled merrily in the warm afternoon air.

That was all it took to set off the devil horse. He screamed and came at the smaller mount again.

"Oh, God. God, please," Celia prayed. She moved faster than she ever had.

The stallion reared and brought his flashing iron-clad hooves down at the pony. She snatched J.J. from the saddle a second before the first hoof indented the leather. The hair stood up on her arm as the hoof fanned by her.

"Get to the house," she ordered the child.

"Mommy. Mommy," he whimpered. He wrapped his arms around her neck.

She turned to see the stallion savage the little pony with a series of bites. The pony turned and delivered a back kick with both hind legs that caught the stallion on one shoulder. The stallion screamed in fury.

Lab tucked tail and ran off a short distance. The pony bumped against Celia. She staggered and tried to step away, but she didn't react fast enough. The two horses reared. The stud overpowered the pony easily, lunging into him and knocking him over.

Celia saw the pony coming. She tore J.J. from her neck and pushed him out of the way. Six hundred pounds of horseflesh brushed against her, catching her bent in a sideways position. She went down, J.J. on top of her. Darkness whirled around her.

She heard J.J. calling her name. Lab growled close to her ear. Herc clambered off and galloped down the road and into the stable. The stallion, after a moment's hesitation, headed for the open road.

Blackness washed over her again. Pain burned her—a hot, tearing sensation deep inside. It racked her in waves across her back. She felt the hot rush of water between her legs. She crawled back from the black abyss.

"J.J., go get your daddy. Ride...the pony." She clenched her hands to stop the cry that rose to her throat when the next wave of pain passed over her. "Get Daddy. Do you understand?" She spoke sternly.

"Yes, ma'am." He took off, Lab loping beside him.

Celia bit down on her lip and held on. The pain was almost solid now, the waves crashing over her without pause.

Curling into a ball on her side, she prayed in short, incoherent bursts. Time became a blur, lost in fear and pain and the pressing darkness that tried to engulf her.

"Marghy," she said to the child inside her. "Don't die."

She heard sounds, someone running, a child's fearful question. "Will Mommy be all right?"

Tom's voice. "Sure, she will. Your little sister's coming a bit early, that's all."

Hunter. Cursing low, fiercely.

She opened her eyes and there it was—that fierce, tender, protective, loving expression—

"Darling, April, darling," he said, as if the words were an incantation, as if they were torn from his soul. "Don't die. Don't you dare die on me," he ordered.

He lifted her into his arms and ran for the truck.

"I'm not—" she tried to tell him, but the pain was there again. The blackness. Rushing at her.

Hunter boosted Celia into the seat, then jumped in and cranked up the engine. "Tell the others," he said to Tom. He looked into his son's terrified eyes. "Tell

Dawn to bring J.J. to the clinic with her. He'll want to be near.''

Tom nodded and slammed the door. Hunter took off as fast as he dared. He didn't want to jostle Celia.

With one hand, he lifted her head into his lap and smoothed the hair from her face. She was deathly white, moans coming from her with each rasping breath.

The stain on her pink shorts had changed to red. He realized she was bleeding. He muttered a savage curse and picked up the cell phone to call ahead.

The staff at the small-town clinic was waiting for them. They whisked her inside and onto an examining table.

Dr. Williamson, who had delivered Hunter, looked into Celia's eyes. ''She's conscious,'' he said.

Hunter nodded.

''What happened?'' the doctor asked as they hooked up an IV and two nurses took Celia's pulse, attached a heart monitor to her and another around her abdomen.

''The pony fell on her. J.J. said there was a horse fight. The stud got out and attacked them.''

Two heartbeats jumped into play on the monitor's screens. One was steady. The other seemed fast.

One of the nurses called out numbers.

''The baby's in distress,'' the doctor explained. ''We'll have to take it.''

''Her,'' Hunter said. ''A girl.''

The medical team worked efficiently, stripping his wife, putting an oxygen clip on her nose. One of them talked softly to her. She did what he said, letting him take blood from her arm. Once, her eyes met Hunter's, then slipped away as if she couldn't focus on one thing for very long.

He was shunted to the side.

"Bleeding," a nurse said.

"Let's go," the doctor replied. "We'll be in surgery," he said to Hunter, giving him a sympathetic smile.

Hunter nodded, but it was to an empty room. The silence closed in. He walked down the hall to the front lobby. The doctor's wife gave him a form to fill out. She told the others who waited that there was an emergency and that they could come back in an hour or they could continue to wait. Everyone stayed.

"Go into the office," she told Hunter.

He went into the doctor's office. He studied the rows of medical books, then sat on the two-section sofa and stared out the window at the lake.

It was slightly over an hour before the doctor returned. "You have a fine girl—five pounds, eleven ounces," he announced with a smile. He slumped into his chair. "Celia hemorrhaged, but we got it stopped. She's stable. She'll be in Recovery for another hour, then we'll move her to a room. You can see her then."

Hunter nodded.

Mrs. Ericson, Dawn, Jackson and J.J. arrived shortly after that. The doctor went to his next patient. Hunter told them the news. J.J. stood beside him. Hunter opened his arms. J.J. climbed into his lap. After a few minutes, he went to sleep.

Hunter held his son to his chest and experienced a rush of love so strong, it hurt. Everything in him hurt.

That first surge of panic when J.J. had ridden up

and told him Mommy was hurt lingered at the edges
of his consciousness.

Not again. Life couldn't do this to him again, had
been his first thought when he'd lifted Celia's curled
body into his arms. He'd flinched at the spasms running through her. He'd heard her gasps of pain, had
known she was holding it in to keep from scaring
their son.

There had been no waiting that other time. April
had been gone when he found her. This time there
was a chance. Celia was strong. She was stubborn.
She'd make it. He clung to that idea while the minutes
crept by.

The nurse brought the baby in and let them see her
for a minute before she went into the incubator to
stabilize her body temperature.

"Hunter, you can go in," the doc's wife told them.
"She's asking for J.J. It would be okay for a minute."

Hunter roused the boy and carried him to Celia's
side. She was awake. Her eyes were tired, but her
smile was bright. He swallowed against the knot in
his throat.

"Hi," she said. She took J.J.'s hand. "Thanks,
sport. You were a real hero. You, too," she said to
Hunter.

He managed a smile. On impulse, he leaned down
and kissed her cheek. J.J. did the same. Her eyes
teared.

"Did you see the baby?" she asked.

"For a minute." He hesitated. "She's beautiful.
Like her mom."

J.J. looked at him in amazement. "Yeah, but she's
skinnier than a plucked chicken," he declared, repeating one of Tom's sayings.

Celia laughed, then sighed. "I think I'd like to sleep now." Fatigue had painted shadows under her eyes.

He nodded. "We'll see you later."

In the waiting room, he arranged for J.J. to stay with Grandma Ericson while he stayed at the clinic. "I don't know if I'll be home tonight. It's according to how she does."

Dawn touched his arm in understanding. She gazed into his eyes for a minute, tilted her head thoughtfully, then smiled as if just discovering a secret.

"What?" he asked.

"Nothing." She lifted J.J. into her arms. "How about we make Uncle Jackson take us to dinner in town?"

"At the hot-dog place?"

"Right. We'll bring you back something before we head out to the ranch," she said to Hunter.

An hour later, they stopped by again and handed him a bag of sandwiches, fries and a drink. When he reported that Celia was still sleeping, they chatted while he ate, then left.

He returned to his wife's room and found that the baby had been moved in with her. Watching Celia's sleep-composed face, he shook his head at how young she looked—a girl on the verge of waking into womanhood, not old enough to have given birth to the child lying close by.

Reliving the moments it had taken to get to her, to touch her and know she still lived, his heart clenched anew.

He pulled his chair closer to the bed and took her hand in his. Such a small hand. Such a big heart.

She'd come to him six months ago with her news,

eyes shining with that expectant glow she had, as if life promised only good things and she believed it. He wished he could give her that moment again. Instead, he'd destroyed it with his anger and doubts, and most of all, with his guilt.

He still didn't have a clear picture of that night, except for those hands that had held and caressed him, that had guided him into the incredible warmth....

Pressing her hand to his chest, he vowed to make it up to her—this woman who had taken him on in spite of his boneheaded refusal to meet her halfway.

Once, he'd thought he was king of his little world. The gods had shown him otherwise. He'd thought he wouldn't be able to marry again—not after April, his perfect love.

Now... Now he saw marriage differently. It could be a partnership. Celia wasn't perfect. She was afraid of cows, horses and strange dogs. She hated confrontations. She was wary of him.

But—he was almost certain of this—she cared for him. And he'd learned to care for her.

He pressed a kiss into her palm and closed her hand around it. "Hold that thought," he whispered, feeling kind and expansive and truly optimistic about their future for the first time.

Celia woke during the night. With the nurse's help, she fed the baby, holding her daughter tucked into the curve of her body as the child learned to nurse. After several tries, Marghy latched on and sucked hungrily.

"I haven't heard her cry," she said, worried about this for some reason.

"She hollered once or twice while she was in the incubator," the nurse told her. "I think she's going

to be one of those good babies who can take the world
as it comes.''

"A wise decision,'' Hunter said.

The nurse greeted him, then bustled out.

Celia met his gaze. She returned his smile. All the
while, her heart was breaking.

He sat on the bed, his big, warm hand on her knee
as their child finished nursing. He even burped the
baby before putting her back in the bassinet.

"How do you feel?'' he asked, returning to her.

"Fine.''

It hurt to look at him, this man who could handle
insane horses and newborns, whether calves or human
babies, without a blink. All in a day's work.

The sadness washed through her. For him. For their
child. For J.J. For April who would never know what
a special son she had, who would never again feel
the tender, powerful, fierce, passionate embrace of the
man who loved her with all his heart.

"Can I get anything for you?'' he asked.

She shook her head.

He bent and kissed her, then returned to the chair
where he'd been sleeping.

"You don't have to stay.''

"Jackson and the men can take care of the ranch
for a couple of days. I'm staying here.'' He settled a
blanket over his long body, smiled at her, yawned and
closed his eyes.

She watched him sleep while darkness seeped into
her soul. She wondered if he'd realized, in those moments after she was injured and on that long drive to
town, that he'd called her April each time he spoke.

Because of honor and duty, he'd felt compelled to

marry her once he'd accepted he was the father of her child, but she wasn't the wife he wanted.

Second choice? She wasn't even that.

Hunter would never have chosen her in a hundred years but for the circumstances of New Year's Eve—his deep loneliness, her absurd request…the unfortunate alignment of the stars; an unkind fate.

The pain of never being wanted for herself burned in her heart. For her, it didn't matter so much, she was used to it; but for her daughter…

A fierce, protective love swelled in her. Her child deserved to come into the world sure of her welcome. Home should be a place to grow in, a place where a child was wanted and loved, secure in her parents' love for her and for each other.

Celia wouldn't allow her child to be raised with the insecurity she'd known all her growing years.

For now, Hunter was kind, but what if he grew to resent her and their daughter? What if he fell in love with someone and wanted her the way he'd wanted April? What if he simply grew tired and couldn't bear to have her around anymore?

She smoothed the white-blond hair on the baby's head, overwhelmed by love for this one tiny, perfect creature.

"I'll never let you be hurt," she promised in a fierce whisper. "No one will make you feel unwanted."

Pressing a hand to her heart, she fought the useless tears and the regret for all the pain she might have caused by her one foolish, selfish act of passion.…

Chapter Fourteen

Celia closed her blouse, burped the baby, then held the infant against her breast. The clock on the mantel ticked off the minutes of the early morning. It wasn't yet six. In order not to disturb Hunter's rest, she'd left her bed when the baby had cried at two that morning, then at four. She'd dressed and stayed downstairs after that, snoozing on the sofa when Marghy wasn't demanding attention.

The house creaked in a friendly fashion as the breeze swept down the mountain and caressed the eaves. She settled more comfortably on the cushions and closed her eyes while idly considering the occupants of the house.

Hunter's mother slept in the downstairs bedroom. She'd returned from her cruise a few days ago, eager to meet the wife her son had married so hastily and to hold the new grandchild. While Mrs. McLean had a reserved attitude toward her, Celia had to admit the woman had clearly fallen in love with her granddaughter. Her mother-in-law held the baby at every opportunity.

J.J., with a little boy's enthusiasm, energetically played with his sister or asked a thousand questions on infant care one minute, then dashed off to play with Lab or follow his father or uncle the next. His acceptance of the baby had been gratifying.

Hunter helped tend his daughter with the sure hand of one experienced in infant needs. He seemed to care very much for their child. Celia was grateful for that.

However, in some ways his caring made the prospect of leaving that much harder to bare. She shied from thinking about it at the moment—

The baby was lifted from her. Hunter smiled and cuddled their daughter against his chest. Celia smiled wearily.

"Restless night?" he asked. He handed her a steaming cup of coffee.

"Yes. Did we wake you?" She cast him an apologetic glance before sipping the hot brew.

He gave a quick shake of his head and sat beside her on the sofa. "I wouldn't have minded. Why don't we take turns at night? I can give her a bottle. That way, you'll have an uninterrupted eight hours of sleep."

She didn't know what to say. She had never expected him to take an active part in raising the child. Actually, she hadn't expected him to take part at all.

"You're quiet," he said, his tone dropping to a

lower register. "You've been quiet for six weeks. Since Marghy was born, in fact."

"I'm fine." But her heart lurched at his words, an accusation she thought.

"But there's a difference. You don't dither anymore. You don't explain yourself into a tangle. You're quiet."

Was this the time to tell him what had been on her mind since that frightening day the baby had been born?

"Maybe we should talk," she began.

She glanced at the clock. It was early. J.J. and her mother-in-law wouldn't be up for another hour. There was time.

"Start with your checkup yesterday."

"Oh. I'm okay…that is, everything is back to normal and I can resume normal activities."

The blush swept into her face a second before the darkness overtook her again. Dear God, why was life so hard?

"Then what's wrong? Don't try to lie. You're terrible at it."

She tried to summon an indignant air, but couldn't. She stared into her cup. How to begin. She sighed softly.

The sadness that had permeated her days since the birth flooded her. She had a terrible need to weep. Postpartum depression, presumably, she told herself in an attempt to dispel it.

No, she had to face the truth. It would break her heart to leave here. She hadn't wanted to love Hunter. She'd tried so hard to guard against it, but to no avail.

"I'm so sorry," she finally said. "I never meant to

interfere in your life. I only wanted— I thought, as adults, we could handle the situation. Instead, everything is hopelessly mixed-up.''

Glancing at him, she was taken all over again by how wonderful he was. She'd learned so much about this man during their months together. He had been very kind to her and sweetly attentive to the baby.

''Go on.''

She shook her head. ''I don't know how to fix it.''

This was getting too serious. She forced a smile, the one that always popped up on her face when she was trying to make the best of a bad situation, when she was nervous—or afraid....

Hunter smiled back. He looked almost tender.

Encouraged, she continued. ''I've made a mess of all our lives. I love J.J., and I think he cares for me—''

''He loves you.''

She nodded. ''I can't bear to leave him.''

''Why should you?'' His tone hardened. The smile was replaced by a frown that wasn't tender at all.

''Well, the baby is born now. And legitimate. So...so my reputation is sterling, and I can get my teaching certificate and support us.''

A strange light gleamed in his eyes. ''Ah, that's generous of you, offering to take on two children, a husband and a mother-in-law on a teacher's salary. However, the ranch is doing okay. I've been meaning to show you where the books are. I thought you could help me keep up with the paperwork, maybe put it on your computer.''

She sighed miserably. ''That isn't what I meant.''

''What do you mean?''

"We can get a divorce—"

"Divorce is out."

Her composure faltered at the flat-out statement. "We have to."

"Why?"

"So you can be free."

"No."

He gave her such a stubborn, gimlet-eyed stare, she was momentarily startled. Her temper frayed. She was trying to be decent and practical about this whole messed-up affair—marriage—whatever.

"We could share custody of Marghy, and I thought... Maybe you wouldn't mind..."

"I would."

"You don't know what I was about to say."

"Shh," he said when the baby roused and puckered up. "There, there," he murmured. He took the sleeping child to the nursery and returned. "How about some breakfast?"

Celia followed him out to the kitchen. Each of them padded about in a pair of tube socks. They looked married and ridiculously normal.

"What's bothering you?" he demanded. He popped waffles into the toaster, found the bottle of syrup and poured big glasses of milk for each of them.

"Us." She sighed. "I don't know what to do."

"Give it a rest."

"What about the divorce?"

"There isn't going to be one. Do you want bacon or sausage or ham?"

"Ham is leaner."

"Fine." He peeled two slices of cooked ham from

the package and slapped it onto a plate, his movements angry. He heated the meat in the microwave.

"Why isn't there going to be a divorce?"

Hunter peered into the refrigerator until he found the tub of margarine. He set it on the counter and turned to study his wife. She perched on the chair, her face earnest and her eyes... Ah, God, she had the most honest eyes of anyone he'd ever known. It had taken him a while to see it.

And to appreciate her, this woman who had brought hope and brightness into his life and that of his son at a time when both of them had desperately needed it.

It came to him that this was love.

The discovery wasn't the blinding light he'd experienced with April, but something softer, like the dawn's breaking, it settled over him like a sigh or a blessing.

The inescapable truth was, he couldn't imagine life without this woman in it.

He'd become addicted to her bright hope that life was going to be wonderful any moment now, to her unshakable belief that, if they were kind to each other, all would be well. He'd come to believe it, too.

It scared him, this need for another person. But it also made life worthwhile. Like the sun rising above the mountain peaks, it lit his soul with love and knowledge.

"Because I can't live without you," he said with total candor.

"That...that doesn't make any sense." She shifted on the limed-oak chair, tension in every line of her small, shapely body. "I've been nothing but trouble since New Year's Eve."

He knew it bothered her that he couldn't exactly recall that night and that she felt guilty, as if she'd taken advantage of him. He smiled upon realizing how well he knew her and how much there was still to be learned. He wanted years to do it. "Well, love has never made much sense, but there you have it." He shrugged as if it was one of life's inescapable foibles.

"You don't," Celia began, then stopped when he turned to her, his eyes ablaze with emotions she couldn't quite trust herself to read.

The next thing she knew he was in her face, his hands at either side of her, trapping her between the chair and his big, masculine body.

"Don't I?" he said, his voice deeper, huskier.

"I..."

"The devil horse is gone. He's history."

"Your prize stud?" She was stunned.

The waffles popped up. He fixed their plates and brought them and silverware to the table. "Nothing on this ranch is worth your life or that of our son and daughter. You can't leave. J.J. loves you."

The switch in subjects made her dizzy.

"Eat," he ordered. "You need nourishment to nurse a child. You're losing weight."

She did as ordered. Each time she looked his way, he was watching her, his eyes a sort of flaming green with hints of gold, flecked here and there with light brown. She was terribly aware of him, of his scrutiny, of the alarms that jangled inside her. The situation was beyond her experience and control.

When she'd eaten every bite under his watchful eye, he cleaned up the kitchen. They were no nearer a solution to their problems that she could see.

"Hunter, it isn't good to sweep problems under the rug. Marriage counselors advise bringing them into the open—"

"You been to a marriage counselor?"

"No, but I've read about it."

"You read a lot." Admiration lit his eyes. "But sometimes you have to close the book and experience life." He lifted her to her feet, then swept her into his arms. "Like now," he suggested in a sexy tone.

"What are you doing?"

He carried her to their bedroom and closed the door. "Making love to my wife. My very beautiful, my foolish, my very brave wife. Every time I see those hoof marks in the pony's saddle, I'm thankful all over again that I have you and J.J. and our daughter, all three of you alive and well. I'll never forget what you did that day."

"Oh, well, that was nothing. I mean, anyone would have. I was terrified," she finished lamely.

"That makes it all the more wonderful."

His gaze confused her. He unbuttoned her top and stripped her of her clothing, then tucked her into bed. He tossed off his jeans and shirts and socks.

Suddenly it was too much—his kindness, the tenderness, the admiration. Tears filled her eyes. She was going to cry. Oh, no. She swallowed hard, then managed a smile. "Don't."

"I have to." He bunched the pillows behind them and cuddled her against his chest. "I need you."

"Oh."

"I love you."

The tears spurted out before she could stop them. She shook her head. "No, you don't. You're grateful, but you don't love me."

He lifted her face and wiped her cheeks with the corner of the sheet. "Why don't I love you?"

"You called me April," she explained, sorry for him and for herself, for their marriage, which shouldn't have been and the one he'd lost. "When you picked me up and put me in the pickup...and on the way to the clinic."

"Ah." He keep sopping up the silly tears. "I think that was because my heart was trying to tell me what it already knew—that I was in love with you."

She couldn't stop the doubts from showing.

"I love April and I'll never forget our time together," he said on a sad note. "But when I look at you, I realize I'm the luckiest man in the world. I lost one love, but I've found another, one just as true. You do love me, don't you?"

"Well..." It took more courage than she realized.

"I love you," he coaxed. "It gets easier after the first time. I'd like to hear you say it."

"I... Love hasn't worked very well for me," she felt compelled to explain.

"I know the feeling." He smiled at her.

It was tender...but sort of fierce, too...and passionate...yes, definitely passionate.

Fires burst into roaring conflagrations at a thousand points inside her and everywhere they touched. She laid her hands on his chest and felt it lift in a deep breath. She felt the air fan warmly across her forehead when he sighed.

"I love you," he said.

"How do you know? When did you know?" She smiled, just in case he took it all back; then she could say she was joking, too.

He grimaced. "It snuck up on me a little at a time. But I knew it when I nearly lost you. At the clinic, waiting to know you and Marghy were okay, I realized how much I cared. Then when you said you were going to leave, it hit me. This is more than caring. This is love. Isn't it?"

She nodded, afraid of this new happiness, afraid it was a trick.

"I loved you first. And the most," he declared in the superior male fashion that infuriated women on general principle.

"Oh, no. I've loved you for ages. All my life. Forever. Tons and tons of— Oh."

He started laughing. "There, that wasn't so bad, was it?"

A river of light flowed inside her. The need to cry dried up. "It was a mean trick."

"Yeah. You're so easy, it's like taking candy from a baby." He licked the tip of her nose and blew on it.

She rubbed the abused part on his chest, then lingered to press her face against him.

He kissed her. She couldn't get her mouth to work right. "Stop smiling," he said.

"I can't."

"Mmm, let's see what I can do about that." He bent his head to her breast and circled it with his tongue, then watched.

A drop of milk appeared. He licked it off, then

gently took the tip into his mouth. Spirals of electricity rushed in all directions. His hands—big, strong, careful hands—clasped her waist, then stroked her back, her hips, her thighs. His smile faded as passion soared.

He made the most exquisite love to her. And he said the words. He was right—it got easier the second and third and fourth times.

Afterward, Hunter held his wife, letting her sleep before they had to rise and take up the chores of the day. He heard J.J. go down the steps, then his mother's voice at the bottom of the stairs. She'd take care of the boy for a while.

He thought Margaret might stay at the ranch after all. Celia had made her feel welcome and wanted in the home that she'd come to as a bride thirty-six years ago.

His wife was like that—a miracle of love that reached out to all who came into her orbit. Including one hardheaded, disbelieving male.

Yes, she was the miracle—the woman who had brought him to life when no other could, who had given him back his son and brought him the gift of a daughter. A miracle.

Thank you.

*   *   *   *   *

We, the undersigned, having barely survived four years of nursing school, do hereby vow to meet at Granetti's at least once a week, not to do anything drastic to our hair without consulting each other first and never, _ever_—no matter how rich, how cute, how funny, how smart, or how good in bed—marry a doctor.

Dana Rowan, R.N.
Lee Murphy, R.N.
Katie Sheppard, R.N.

Christine Flynn
Susan Mallery
Christine Rimmer

prescribe a massive dose of heart-stopping romance in their scintillating new series, **PRESCRIPTION: MARRIAGE**. Three nurses are determined _not_ to wed doctors— only to discover the men of their dreams come with a medical degree!

Look for this unforgettable series in fall 1998:

October 1998: **FROM HOUSE CALLS TO HUSBAND** by Christine Flynn

November 1998: **PRINCE CHARMING, M.D.** by Susan Mallery

December 1998: **DR. DEVASTATING** by Christine Rimmer

Only from

Silhouette®SPECIAL EDITION®

Available at your favorite retail outlet.

COMING NEXT MONTH